Minds Above Water

A collection of poetry and prose

Russell Partridge

The Cloister House Press

ISBN 978-1-909465-07-7

First published in the United Kingdom in 2013
by The Cloister House Press

Contents

POETRY

PLAY

A NEW PARISH

The Reverend Michael Potts took the ladle and gave the thick soup a purposeful stir as it stood on the warming plate. Teresa Coles was halving home-made brown rolls and buttering them with aplomb. Six men, five of them with bushy beards, and a rather dishevelled looking young woman sat on red plastic chairs around two tables with plain white tablecloths. They sat in silence spooning hot soup gingerly through cracked lips.

Suddenly an angry looking man in his fifties bustled and bundled his way through the double doors of the church hall. He came to a halt, centre stage, in the middle of the hall and gesticulated at the Reverend Potts.

"You should spend a bit more time looking after your church-going parishioners than these lazy drop-outs," he announced.

"Be that as it may," replied Michael. "But the Lord Jesus cared for the unfortunate." The man waved his hand wildly and continued, "We're paying your wages. You've done nowt about the church roof. This lot don't pay council tax!"

"The church roof will get seen to in good time, these people do not always have a roof over their heads," replied Michael in a typically measured tone.

The man was flabbergasted and enraged by Michael's calm response, but feeling the pangs of an imminent defeat, marched towards the exit pushing aside an elderly man who was coughing and trying to blow his nose at the same time. The doors banged shut as David Walker exited the hall with a defiant flourish. The old man shuffled into a vacant chair and was served with a bowl of steaming soup by the Reverend Potts himself.

Marjorie Baker put on her woollen hat and gloves and stepped out into the strengthening March sunlight with her dog. The early frost was still evident on the shady verges of the main street. Birds chattered and flitted in the leafless limes. Her attention was drawn to the fiery David Walker walking briskly towards her with long strides.

"Hello, David."

"Marjorie, that new pain of a vicar is really winding me up with all his do-gooding."

"I'm inclined to agree with you," replied Marjorie trying to placate him.

"Why won't he do what's important for the parishioners instead of doling out soup to dropouts?"

"Yes, I was only talking to Jane Ross yesterday. She wants to see the back of him, her husband too."

"I suppose we could petition the bishop."

"You could. But I'd leave it a few weeks, he might get the message by then. You know what they say, 'A new broom sweeps clean.'"

David shrugged reluctantly. They went on their way.

"I see Teresa Coles creeping around Potts again," said Ethel Rhodes to the post-mistress as she collected her pension on Monday morning.

"Do you think there's something going on there?" replied Wendy Hughes.

"Wouldn't be surprised. Teresa hasn't had a fling in years far as I know. He'd make my skin creep."

"If it weren't for her I think he would have been gone long since," said Wendy counting out the notes brusquely.

Michael Potts allowed himself one little pleasure outside pastoral duties and functions and that was a National Lottery ticket which he bought from the local shop every Friday afternoon. Michael was a dignified man, self-assured and courteous and he would chat with ordinary folk in the queue. Further back in the queue that day were Jessica Holmes and Paula Relph, both of whom were pregnant.

"Not above buying a lottery ticket is 'e," whispered Jessica.

"Yeh, I bet he'll buy some for Teresa," giggled Paula.

"What condoms or lottery tickets!" They sniggered quietly.

The Reverend Potts sat in his study that Saturday evening writing his sermon for morning prayer the next day. This he found the most difficult aspect of his ministry. He was not a man for big evangelical outbursts but wanted deeply to inspire his congregation. He had written most of it but now looked pensively through the study window at the daffodils but without really seeing them, for want of a new idea. He began to feel restless and decided to go into the lounge to watch the National Lottery draw and return to his sermon later.

Five minutes later a surprisingly calm and collected Michael phoned Teresa.

"I think I might have won the jackpot on the lottery, Teresa."

"Oh! How wonderful Michael. Hey, maybe we could take a holiday together, that would get the tongues wagging."

"I'll need to think about it. I think we'll need to fix the church roof but the bishop will probably insist that it comes out of diocesan funds."

"Oh, you! You always have to think about things," she teased kindly.

The next day morning prayer was poorly attended. Marjorie Baker was just about there with six others. The Reverend Potts gave a sermon with which he was pleased, perhaps his best since he had arrived six months ago. Nevertheless, when all had gone he held some despondency and introspection about the difficulties of running a new parish. He was so very grateful for Teresa's continued loyalty. She had been in church today.

By Wednesday, everyone in Swelbury knew of Michael Potts's good fortune as his picture appeared on the front page of *The Post* holding a cheque for £7 million with the headline "Local Vicar Scoops Jackpot". Michael was glad when all the photographs and chit-chat was over and he could get on with his job. The phone never stopped ringing all week with messages of congratulations, genuine or otherwise.

On Thursday morning there was a knock at the rectory door. Michael opened it to find Jessica Holmes and Paula Relph standing beaming at him.

"Congratulations vicar."

"Thank you," said Michael in his usual measured tone.

"We would like to ask you a small favour," said Jessica pulling her hair back behind her ear. "Would you be able to spare a little money for the mothers and toddlers group and the playgroup?"

"All I can say is I need to think about it," replied Michael.

Later on Thursday evening, while Michael and Teresa were chatting in the lounge, there was another louder knock on the door. Again without displaying irritation Michael opened the door. Standing at the door in bright moonlight were Jane Ross, Marjorie Baker and her dog.

"We've just popped round to say hi and well done."

"Thank you."

"We were wondering whether you might be kind enough to help pay for repairs to the church roof," persuaded Marjorie with her characteristic self-confidence and audacity.

"You are not the first people to suggest it to me. In theory it's a good idea but Bishop Martin feels that it should come from diocesan funds."

Their faces flopped at that.

"Oh well, we'll try and make it on Sunday won't we Jane?"

"That would be good, there were only a few there last week weren't there, Marjorie?"

On Friday afternoon Michael could forgo his visit to the shop and he decided to visit three sick parishioners in order to offer them Holy Eucharist and talk to them. When he returned he was genuinely tired of having to say thank you to everyone's congratulations. He had resolved firmly to continue working. He walked slowly through the front door and observed a note on the doormat. He stooped to pick it up.

"Sorry I was so offhand with you vicar. The Rotary Club is a bit short of money now.

I know you enjoy coming along. If you could possibly help out it would be much appreciated. Yours, David."

On the next Sunday, Michael was genuinely surprised at the size of his congregation.

David Walker, Jane Ross, Jessica Holmes, Paula Relph, Ethel Rhodes, Wendy Hughes and all their spouses and children arrived smartly dressed. Marjorie Baker offered to read from the Bible. One absentee was Teresa, who was visiting a friend. Because of this Michael felt nervous before giving his sermon and ended up giving the worst account of himself yet. There were no disparaging comments however and everyone shook hands with him afterwards but the Reverend Potts could see through their eyeless smiles.

That evening the Reverend Michael Potts sat in his study as the twilight faded and Venus began to light the western sky. Thoughtfully and very deliberately he withdrew his cheque book and two envelopes from his desk drawer.

Pay Miss T. Coles one million pounds only.

Pay Shelter four million pounds only.

For the Lord sees the good deeds you do in secret.

AFTER ALL THESE YEARS

I live at Holly Cottage. At the side of the garden there are three sturdy holly trees in the hedge that separates me from the Wilkins next door. They're a pleasant couple and come round occasionally for coffee with their daughter Theresa when she is visiting them. Theresa is an accountant, she is Bob and Sue's only child and they are immensely proud of her. She always dresses smartly and is very prim and proper but I wouldn't invite her to a dance, sorry to say. I've never seen her let her hair down, nor can I imagine her doing so. They are here with me now, the day before I go to look at the place of my birth for the first time in my adult life. You might ask why I've left it so long but my Dad kept silent about the circumstances of my birth even to his grave five years ago. I've had to rely on the deductive skills of my elder sister Ruth and she and I don't always get on. My friend Charlotte, or Lottie as I know her, is taking me the fifty miles to Rothford tomorrow. Lottie is quite bubbly and cheerful and does wonders for my self-confidence. Don't get me wrong, Theresa is a good friend but I don't think she could do the emotional stuff with me so I haven't asked her.

"How's the painting going?"asked Bob after I had hung up their coats. It is a bitter January day.

"So, so. I did a watercolour over the Christmas holiday of Edinburgh Castle. I'll show it to you in a minute. It's the first I've done for ages."

"No hurry," said Bob. Bob is a photographer and we share an interest in visual arts.

"Are you alright Alice?" said Sue. "You seem very tense."

"I'm uptight about this trip tomorrow, to be honest, I'm going to my birthplace."

"We understand Alice, we remember you telling us last month," said Theresa shaking my hand rather formally.

The Wilkins stayed an hour but we really didn't get above polite chit-chat apart from positive comment about my watercolour. I slept fitfully that night, I've always been of a nervous disposition. Several times I got out to lie on the top of the bed to rotate my ankles, fidget and stretch my legs. I nipped down to the kitchen to warm some milk in the microwave. The tick of the kitchen clock was the only sound in the enveloping darkness of a cloudy January night. Two fourteen flashed on the microwave clock as it pinged and I grasped my milk.

Lottie arrived in her grey *Ford Focus* spot on ten as arranged. I darted out of the door having double-checked that everything was locked or turned off.

"Nice smell in here," I said as Lottie pulled away smoothly.

"It's these tree deodorants," said Lottie changing gear and drawing up at the junction at the end of our road.

"It's so good of you to take me. I don't know how I'll feel when we get there."

"It's good that you feel a lot after all these years. You really care what happened."

We sat in silence for five minutes. My eyelids began to droop as we travelled along a fast piece of dual-carriageway.

"Ruth went last year. Apparently the place was still a building site."

"I passed by last November on a work visit to Rothford and the builders had finished. It was all looking pretty ship-shape."

Small raindrops began to spatter the windscreen. Lottie clicked on the windscreen wipers. Initially the rubber grated but soon they were swishing away heavy rain, grime and brown saltiness.

"Only about twenty minutes and we're there," said Lottie sensing my unease.

As we approached Rothford the rain suddenly stopped, the sky cleared to the north-west and the car windows steamed up as the temperature dropped. We turned up a steep side road with water gushing down either gulley as a watery beam of sunlight cut across the clouds. In front was a large gated entrance before a big imposing building.

"Here we are. Plock Hill House," said Lottie. Unable to quell my immediate curiosity I slipped out, before Lottie parked up, to survey the magnificent structure.

Grand red brickwork supported large bay-windows. The Tudor chimney stacks remained and there was a large imposing oak door which seemed to lead on to a lighted vestibule.

"It's luxury flats," said Lottie softly, obviously waiting to gauge my reaction.

"Mum was one of the last patients to leave the sanatorium, so Ruth told me."

"Really."

We walked slowly round the building dodging the puddles and kerbside enclaves where trees fought the winter chill.

"Ruth said I was two weeks early and Mum gave birth to me six days before leaving. It must have been a hard time for her."

"It must have."

We walked around the back of the building. There was a pile of dead Christmas trees at the refuse collection point awaiting disposal. This sight seemed to deepen my ensuing melancholy.

"You're thoughtful," offered Lottie.

"Yes," I murmured. "Ruth told me Mum passed away when I was eighteen months."

I paused, took a deep breath to hold back a tear.

"I feel odd coming here."

"I expected you would."

"It being luxury flats now. Seems to betray what Mum suffered here with the other women."

"I think she would have been happy really with the hospital closing down, TB was a real scourge."

"But the place is part of our family history, I was never old enough to talk to Mum about it and Dad must have felt guilty about it. He kept quiet."

"Yes but your Aunty May used to visit when she was allowed. She could tell you more."

"She's a bit of an old stick now, I don't feel like bothering her much. She told me a bit four years ago when she came over to stay, but she was so demanding that I didn't invite her back."

The sun illuminated the brickwork giving it an orange glow. I pulled out my ageing digital camera, took three flash snaps and ambled sombrely back to Lottie's car.

Often I think about Mum, especially when I'm knitting children's clothing. Would she be proud of me after all these years?

AMMONITE

"What's this?"

"Sausages, we're going on holiday."

"And who are they for, we're vegetarians?"

"I thought the kids would like a treat."

"Oh really, I thought we were agreed we're all vegetarians now. Terrible cruelty goes on to animals you know."

"O.K. We'll give them to Bruce for when he's at Maggie's."

"No. Bruce is vegetarian too now."

"Since when?"

"Last Wednesday. You remember a parcel of veggie dog food came in the post. I told you."

"Sorry I'd forgotten it came while I was at work, you could have reminded me. Don't you think this is getting silly?"

"No, not at all, there's loads of nice veggie stuff in *Viva*'s catalogue, I was even thinking of becoming a vegan."

"Vegan food is too expensive. It will cost us a small fortune to keep all four of us and Bruce fed."

"There are nice cheap recipes in the magazines, you can get vegan shoes and clothes too."

"The time you'll take to cook them you will be a full-time housewife, my salary won't cover the bills."

"I've been thinking, there are a few vegan guesthouses around the country. May be I could stay at home and let out the cottage to vegan guests. They would probably keep it cleaner and respect it because their needs are being catered for. The students were noisy and left chip wrappers and about a dozen dirty mugs lying around last time I cleaned."

"That sounds a good idea but we'll need to advertise pretty widely in the vegetarian press."

Lucy and James gambolled in noisily in their wellingtons followed by Maggie, a friend of Paul and Christine. Maggie of sanguine character had thick curly auburn hair tied back at the nape. She wore a thick, green, woollen cardigan and soft casual trousers inside her wellingtons.

"Maggie showed us the little stream in the valley at Brampton," said Lucy throwing her coat on the floor. James did likewise and said "We tried to dam the stream with stones Mum. In the end it fell down but before there was a pool of water right up to the top of our wellingtons."

"Could you hang your coats on the hooks darlings and take off your wellies by the door.

"Have they worn you out Maggie? Is it still alright for you to look after Bruce when we go on Saturday? Paul's a member of UNISON and we're going to stay at their holiday centre at Croyde Bay, it's near Ilfracombe. Would you like a ginger and lemon with us?"

"No I won't stop, I've a lot of marking to do for my students. But thank you all the same."

Bruce was aroused by the smell of mud and padded out into the hall to sniff the children's wellingtons thoroughly.

"If you two get changed we're going into Melksham on the bus in half an hour," said Paul.

"O.K. Dad."

The children clattered and bumped their way upstairs still excited by their morning of fun with Maggie.

Paul poured himself a glass of red grape juice, ran his hand through his thin fair hair pensively.

"I've been thinking. Won't the children get picked on at school if we send them with vegan lunch boxes, you know what kids are like."

"At least they'll have each other at lunchtime and anyway I think it would be good to send them to Briars Steiner School before long, if I can get the guest house up and running with my savings."

"Yeh, but would it be filled all the year round? How many vegans are there around?"

"Quite a few these days."

"How long have you been thinking this through?"

"When we were sitting outside the Apple Tree café last Monday."

"I'm going to have to get promotion or a better paid job, while you get started. We'll need to redecorate the cottage. I think they demand disabled access these days, there's only steps to the cottage door."

"We could put a ramp in at the back and a lift. Think positive."

"This is still sounding too expensive to me."

"When it's up and running and the children are in their teens I could do some freelance writing from home."

"That's a long way off. That Steiner school will cost a bomb. Aren't we happy as we are?"

"Speak for yourself. Childcare is alright but I would like to branch out and use my adult brain a bit. You come home so late I barely speak to another adult some days and you're always tired."

"I know love … let's go into town."

"Lucy, James, are you ready?" Christine shouted from the bottom of the stairs.

"I've lost my hairband, Mum. Can you help me look for it?"

"Don't worry love," said Christine ascending the stairs. "Just brush your hair and it will look lovely."

"But Mum, I want my hairband, it was here this morning."

James ran down the stairs in his new training shoes smiling at his father Paul, who was combing his hair before the long mirror in the hall.

"Have you got your purse James? I'm wanting you to be more grown up and bring your pocket money with you to town."

"I've got my purse Daddy but there's only a bit of money in it. Lucy and me bought that beach ball remember and I paid for most of it."

"Of course I remember. Soon you'll be able to count it out when you've done your sums at school. Lucy, Christine, are you ready?"

There was the sound of light sobbing and rummaging upstairs.

Bruce bounded into the hall barking at the sound of his lead being taken from the understairs cupboard. He jumped up on to Paul's thighs and wagged his tail violently.

"We've found it. Just coming." Christine and Lucy bounded down the stairs.

"The bus leaves in seven minutes, so we'd better hurry," said Paul as Bruce strained on his lead.

*

Six days later the family were enjoying an afternoon in Ilfracombe. The sun shone diffusely through high cirrus cloud and there was a light sea-breeze to temper the warmth. There was plenty of activity in the harbour and the circling seagulls were vociferous.

"Perhaps we could stroll around the harbour and then go around the shops," said Paul.

Lucy was all for going straight to the shops as she had saved her £5 pocket money.

"I'd like to go on a boat trip on that blue boat," said James.

"It's rather expensive darling, we'll see what money we have left on Friday and perhaps go then if the weather's fine," said Christine.

James started to whine but was chided by his father. The family mooched along the harbour exchanging nods with the boat owners. Paul and Christine linked arms and chatted happily. The children were unusually quiet and a little disgruntled until Christine spotted a quaint looking gift shop selling minerals and fossils on the other side of the harbour.

"O.K. kids we'll cross over and go in there. I know you're busting to go to the shops."

Lucy's and James's spirits lifted quickly. The shop was compact but beautifully laid out and bustling with tourists.

"When you're a vegan you won't be able to buy these fossils," Paul teased his wife.

"They lived a natural life. The children might love a couple," retorted Christine fondling an ammonite tenderly with her right hand while resting it on her left.

"We'd like one of these each," said Lucy intrigued by the pleasant symmetry of the ammonites, running her index finger along each of the grooves in the fossil's shell.

"Yes," cried James, animated.

"How much are they?" said Lucy boldly to the genial and laid-back shopkeeper.

"Five pounds each."

"Ah," said Christine. "Lucy give me £2 and I'll pay the rest, because you might want an ice-cream before we leave and pocket money day is tomorrow. James give me a pound towards yours."

"That's not fair," protested Lucy. "Just because I've saved my money I have to pay more than him."

"James spent more on the beach ball, if you remember, so why don't we go down to the beach now. I'll choose a couple of postcards for Aunty May and Uncle Raymond and perhaps you can write them when we get back to the chalet. I'll buy something for Maggie for looking after Bruce and you two can give me fifty pence each towards it."

The sun began its late summer decline in the western sky, hazy and orange in the bank of cirroform cloud. It became cooler and the sea-breeze died away to calm.

Lucy and James played happily on the small beach in front of the sea wall with their new multicoloured plastic ball. Paul looked on with serene contentment at his two boisterous but lovely children, sated by the interlude away from thoughts of future financial worries. Christine bought two postcards and a tin of biscuits from what was a very tacky shop compared with the fossil shop. She paced urgently across a zebra crossing not really wanting to be far from Lucy and James. She trusted Paul throughout but because she spent most of her waking hours with the children there was a slight churning in the pit of her stomach at having to leave them for more than a few minutes. If she were to run the guest house she would have to be strong and overcome this as the children grew up. She knew things were going to be difficult despite the softening of Paul's attitude to her beliefs about the sanctity of life and her impending veganism.

Paul and Christine had saved hard for their week's holiday at the UNISON holiday centre at Croyde Bay. The facilities were pleasant without being extravagant. They arrived back at their family chalet at 8.30pm by which time the musicians were tuning up for the nightly entertainment in the main hall. Sound checks and gruff men's voices boomed out into the cool crepuscular air, stars were beginning to appear in the clear eastern sky. There was a thudding of balls on rackets as two accomplished tennis players rounded off a set before dark. The stillness allowed the completion of a game of badminton on the lawn surrounded on four sides by pristine white chalets. Lucy and

James wrote their postcards yawning loudly, their eyelids drooping after a long day.

"It's a bit risky to go out now," said Christine on returning from giving the children their goodnight hugs and kisses.

"Yep, maybe you're right, there's a matinee tomorrow we could all go to."

Christine kissed her husband tenderly on the cheek and laid her right hand across his strong spine as they embraced. He enjoyed the warmth of her chest on his.

"I hope Bruce is O.K. with Maggie," said Christine. They all missed their ebullient Collie cross who was so good with the children, now they were less timid with him.

Christine and Paul watched darkness envelope the holiday centre as the gibbous moon rose in the east. There was a low murmur of conversation punctuated with hoots of laughter.

The couple sipped their chamomile and spearmint tea while sitting in the green lawn chairs assigned to their chalet. They didn't hear James stir from his bed and pad quietly to his wardrobe and stop and let his eyes get accustomed to the dark. He opened the door, which creaked on its hinges, bent down and reached into the cloth bag. He lifted out the bundle wrapped in tissue paper and carefully removed the paper to reveal the ammonite. He ran his fingers over its contours, rubbed it gently against his cheeks and then turned it over and over with devotional intrigue.

At 9.50pm Christine and Paul were half-way through a game of Scrabble in their room when Paul's mobile phone pealed a tune.

"Hello Maggie."

"Really?"

"Is it serious?"

"Oh."

"They might operate?"

"O.K."

"We'll be back tomorrow afternoon."

"What's going on Paul? Why are we going back tomorrow?"

"It's Bruce. Maggie says he's swallowed a sharp object. The vet says they might have to operate."

Sorrowful that the holiday that they were so looking forward to was to be curtailed after five days Christine checked on Lucy. The light of the moon etched her soft features as she slumbered. Christine pulled the door to now Lucy was fast asleep. Suddenly there was a bump from James's room. Christine jerked open the door a crack to reveal James sitting cross-legged in the middle of his room looking downwards wistfully.

"What are you doing?"

"You don't like hurting animals Mum."

"No, I don't love."

"I d … dropped my anno … annomite. Will he … will he be hurt Mum?"

"Darling, he lived a long time ago."

"D … did a dinosaur kill him?"

"I doubt it Jamie, put him back now and try and sleep."

Two hours later James was dreaming pre-historic dreams.

CRAIG

Craig was always first into the locker room. He liked it that way. The privacy to change his clothes before the chatter began, before the steaming of the communal shower and macho banter created claustrophobia in Craig's quiet introspective mind.

Work began at 8.45am It was spot on 7.20am when Craig stepped out eagerly into the corridor that led to the stairs to the "Fitness Room". Everyone Craig spoke to called it the "Gym" but he insisted on calling it the "Fitness Room". As usual Craig was wearing two red towelling sweat bands around his wrists and a green one around his forehead. He wore clean white socks and underpants and he fiddled with the tie on his shorts as he ascended the stairs.

Craig put the key in the door and pushed it open tentatively. He looked around furtively for anyone who would disturb his reverie while using the treadmill. Usually there wasn't a soul around but this morning Craig had company. A grey-haired balding man was pumping the weights. His grunts became more stifled as Craig entered. Perhaps, mused Craig, here was someone who wanted to grunt as much as he liked. Mostly Craig had great difficulty in appreciating other people's needs but quite out of character he offered a "Good Morning" to the man who reciprocated with a nod and a slight smile. Craig mounted the treadmill, fiddled with the keypads and began to march to the movement under his spanking new trainers. A vague incline of the need to share crossed Craig's mind but he tried to repress it. Craig looked at his watch, 7.47am. Time to start his warm down. At that moment a young man and young woman entered the cool air-conditioned gym. They were chatting softly and from the corner of his eye as he began his warming down exercises, Craig sensed intimacy.

Craig was a little scared of such things.

Craig came to the fitness room daily Monday to Friday, performed his office duties skilfully and dutifully, went home and cooked a microwave meal with steamed vegetables and ate yoghurt for dessert. Every evening at 6.45pm he phoned the most important person in his life, his mother. Craig's mother Margaret lived in his home town of Dornoch, north of Inverness. Craig had moved south to Basildon at the tender age of twenty bringing his computer skills and his attention to detail. He had lost his father in early childhood, was an only child and worried ceaselessly about his mother's health despite her assurances that she was fine. After his daily phone call Craig would settle down with a science-fiction novel, then read computing magazines until ten, when he would watch *The Ten O'Clock News* and turn in. At the weekend, if it was fine, he would play football with Scott and Eddie from work, in the nearby park. He would read, visit the library and watch the occasional film on DVD. On Sunday he would clean the flat fastidiously and wash, dry and iron his clothes ready for the next working week.

Just as Craig began to muse analytically on intimacy, the older man with the bald head stumbled tiredly over to the warm-down mat, stretched, turned and began a yoga routine next to Craig. Craig smelled a whiff of sweat and wrinkled up his nose.

The next morning Craig arrived at the fitness room in a hurry, it was 7.23am, he was three minutes late. He adjusted his sweat bands and fiddled with shorts tie. There was the grey-haired man with the bald head again puffing hard on one of the two treadmills. Craig jumped up on to the other and said "Good morning."

"I'm Terry, you are?"

"Craig."

"You a regular here?"

"Try to be."

"I've just started here."

"Good effort, never too late to start."

"My wife died of a heart attack, only 58. Frightened me a bit. So I decided to come here. Did you send any Valentines?"

Craig turned to him and looked absently.

"Valentines, yeh. It's Saint Valentine's Day today."

"Oh, I didn't realise. Haven't really thought about it."

"What, a young man like you?"

"No. I tend only to read Sci-Fi and computer magazines."

"Ah you need to do a bit of living, young man, like you said, it's never too late to start."

"Eh?"

Craig was about to rebuke Terry for being a romantic old fool when the thought crossed his mind that this treadmill might be a microcosm of his life. His next thought, however, led him to observe that it was already 7.47am and time to warm down. Terry joined him, slightly to Craig's irritation. At the end of the warm-down Terry said:

"How about we go to The Halfpenny for a drink some time? I don't get out too much myself."

"That's a very kind offer Terry but I am really quite busy," said Craig and left the gym. Terry left a little later looking resigned.

That day at work was difficult for Craig. At 10.11am all the computers in the office crashed. It was usually pleasantly quiet on his floor with the comforting whirr of industry. As a cacophony of chatter ensued Craig became quite anxious. He made for the drinks machine where he found himself chatting to a young woman. Craig had never before exchanged more than a fleeting hello to her during her six months at the office. Debbie laughed and joked with him and Craig felt quite light-headed as he looked into her brown eyes with unknown fascination. He sipped from his coffee frequently and began tapping his foot involuntarily. After ten minutes or so Craig thought it was time to check his computer to see whether it was functioning again. Everyone else were busy talking, drinking and laughing around the vending machine but Craig felt a pang of guilt that he wasn't earning his pay. All this frivolity didn't bode well. Very soon, order was restored and everyone returned to their desks reluctantly. Ah, silence at last thought Craig.

After the lunch break Craig returned to his desk at 1.45pm sharp. He could sense a giggly atmosphere among some of the women. He was sure Mark had winked at him on the way in. Usually, the others took little notice of him as he shuffled to focus on his computer. Craig's worktop was as ever very neat and tidy but this afternoon there was in front of him a single red rose and a red envelope. He pushed them to one side and logged on to the system and craned his neck towards the screen. Debbie's friend Sharon arrived at the machine next to Craig's. She looked across and noticed Craig's ignorance of his flower and card.

"Not opening your card then."

"Not in work time. I'll open it at tea break," said Craig disdainfully.

"He's not opened it," said Sharon loudly so that every head in the room turned. Debbie rose from her chair and marched over to Craig's desk.

"Bloody well open it you zombie!"

"Don't call me a zombie and get on with your work."

"You just have no heart at all. It's all up here isn't it," she retorted tapping her head with her finger.

Craig opened the card self-consciously as all eyes bore down on him. He read it.

It was from Debbie. He read it again because at first it didn't sink in.

"I like you a lot," said Debbie softly. "Make us a date, Craig."

Craig stared into space, eyes glazed for a few moment before almost whispering, "Debbie, I haven't been out with a woman before."

"Yeh, but you're always smart, good at your job, nice company."

"O.K. We'll meet at tea break and fix a time."

There was a big cheer around the room as the floor manager, Clive, entered. It all went quiet abruptly.

"What's going on here this afternoon?"

"Oh just a little Valentine's fun," said Sharon trying to suppress a giggle.

"Nothing to do with our friend Craig is it?" said Clive winking at Craig.

"Thank you Clive," said Craig almost doubled up with embarrassment.

"I hope you'll be able to get up for your morning workout now you're with Debbie."

Everyone chuckled and even Craig managed a quick grin.

DO YOU MISS ME?

Angela scowled. It was an expression I'd grown familiar with over the past few weeks.

"Why do you have to go there when I'm scawting around like someone demented trying to keep a roof over our heads?"

"I think I'm due a win, like on the Grand National last year."

"I'm giving you one more week and if you gamble, you're out. Remember the house an' all is in my name."

I had been made redundant from my job as a sheet metal worker ten months ago. At first I had tried to find work but my skills did not match what was on offer. Soon I consoled myself in being a good househusband. It was only when I turned to the odd flutter from my Job Seeker's Allowance and more frequent binges on fruit machines, that Angela turned on me. To be honest, I expected Angela to round on me much earlier when I was doing the cooking, washing, ironing and cleaning. On reflection, she was a reasonable, unprejudiced woman. Many a man's wife would have turned on him much earlier particularly when there were no children or pets to look after at home. I would have liked a dog but Angela insisted the animal would be too much of a tie, especially if we wanted to go on holiday. Not that there was any suggestion of holidays since our week in the Peak District two years ago. We had hired a camper van, walked Dovedale hand in hand, the last time we had ever done so. We visited and marvelled at the Blue John caves at Castleton and explored Buxton. It was almost idyllic because the weather held.

I managed five days of agony and longing to visit the bookies after Angela's last remonstration. I tried to cook a tasty meal for her when she returned from work but the results were barely appetising. Angela said little during those five days. There were no blazing rows. Although she was patient and slow to admonish, she was also sparing with her praise. It was if she was living on autopilot and I felt inspired to do little in response to her level-headedness.

*

On Friday night I slept little. I resolved to rise early, make breakfast and slip out furtively to the bookies whilst doing the shopping. Dutifully I brought Angela breakfast and she seemed a little more appreciative than usual, then I made my escape.

My palms were moist and my heart pounded as I placed my £30 on "Spanish Steps" in the 2.30 at Haydock. I stood to gain £570 if it came in.

When I arrived home, with less shopping than usual, Angela handed me an envelope.

"You'll need to pay some of the council tax, Brian, I can't afford to pay it all. The bill's come today."

"Yes," I said peevishly and slipped off into the kitchen to make myself and Angela a cup of tea.

I started to unpack the shopping and place it in the refrigerator and cupboards. Angela stalked in behind me like a cat ready to pounce.

"That lot isn't going to last us the week," she observed. "Have you been to the bookies?"

I turned my head to face her like a child who knows he has done wrong. The fight had drained out of me. "Yes," I said not catching her eye.

"I really think you ought to leave Brian, I can't take any more of this."

"You're not the only one," I offered.

"Pack your things and leave."

I left with a rucksack of belongings slung over my back. I bought a bottled drink with the little money I had left and sat down on a dedicated bench in the local churchyard.

The sight of the straggly yews seemed to deepen my sadness rather than engage with it. Having eaten the peanut butter sandwiches I had packed, I mooched off to the bookies to watch the race. Usually I felt animated while I watched a race but today my eyes were glazed with misery too great for tears. My horse finished fifth. I would have to find somewhere to sleep knowing that my nearest relative lived thirty miles away in Wolverhampton. I didn't have it in me to walk that far and negotiate the maze of streets in the conurbation.

At sunset I settled down with my sleeping bag in a shop doorway and slept fitfully with a small bean bag as a pillow. I was thankful that no-one harrassed or disturbed me to move me on.

The next morning I was thirsty and it being a Sunday, I decided to slip into the church and attend the service for a free cup of coffee afterwards. I received some odd glances when I put my rucksack next to me in my pew. I have never been particularly religious but the atmosphere in the church grounded me with a sense of peace and tranquillity. There was an ephemeral smell of lilies wafting through the general mustiness. I glanced at the solid candles on the altar burning without a flicker as if to reinforce the agelessness of faith. For a few seconds I wished that my main motive for being here was not to cadge a cup of coffee. The vicar seemed pleasant and I enjoyed singing the hymns. In that hour in the church I became acutely aware of my mortality and the fragility of my existence. I needed to draw on my spirit and found it easier to pray to the Almighty than at any time in my life. I even prayed for Angela.

As the congregation gathered at the end of the service, the vicar and an elderly woman next to him eyed me warily. To my surprise, after a few seconds they approached me and began to chat. I explained my circumstances truthfully.

"There is a hostel in Stafford but unfortunately there are no buses today. Perhaps I could run you over there when we have tidied up and left the church."

The vicar's words were music to my ears and I felt genuine gratitude to him when he dropped me in Stafford town centre forty minutes later. I thanked him from the bottom of my heart.

It took two false starts to find the hostel as people's directions confused me.

"Hello sir, can you spare a bed for the night?"

"Come in. Do you have any identification?"

I had been meticulous about my packing and handed over my passport after some rummaging in my bag. My bed was a bottom bunk in a small room with four bunk beds and wash basin and a little window overlooking the town. At the time of arrival I was the sole occupant. I ripped off my boots, lay down and closed my heavy eyelids. You don't appreciate that which you've never lost I mused as I dozed. The next thing I knew there was a knock on the door and the kindly man who had shown me to my room popped his head round the doorframe and said, "There's a bowl of soup and some sandwiches for you in the dining room."

"Thank you," I drawled sleepily.

I made an effort to move but my body had stiffened since the previous night. I looked at my watch. I had been asleep for two hours. I felt my bones and tendons creak as I swung my legs around and sat on the edge of my bunk, my back arched to avoid banging my head on the top bunk. I yawned and sighed deeply as I stretched and lumbered stuporously to the dining room.

There were two young women and two older men sitting in the dining room. One of the men offered a "Hiya", the others continued eating their sandwiches.

"I'm Brian."

"Peter. Pleased to meet you."

Peter had a copy of the *Big Issue* in front of him.

"I sometimes sell these. Worth giving it a try," he said.

I nodded and sipped my soup and munched my sandwiches in the ensuing silence.

Time passed slowly at the hostel. I spent a lot of time lying on my bed, staring at the upper bunk and weighing up plans for my future. Selling the *Big Issue* seemed like an option. I did pop out from time to time to chat to other residents but the conversations were very stilted. Once or twice I stepped out to the local corner shop in the swirling fog to buy chewing gum and a canned drink, that was all I could afford. But most of the time I lay and thought, thought about the hurt Angela and I had caused each other. I was not as depressed as would seem given my circumstances. Eventually my life had to take a new direction after ten months of stagnation, even if it had tenuous new beginnings.

*

I stayed four nights at the hostel before I was politely moved on to look for accommodation.

Nowadays, I have a small bedsit in Stafford. I receive enough Benefit to buy a little food and pay my rent. I stand in the rain, piercing cold and stifling heat selling copies of the *Big Issue* in Stafford town centre. The same place I stand six days a week.

I have a little dog, Pat, to keep me company and many friends and acquaintances stop by and chat. Some give me money without taking a magazine. Pat receives biscuits and meaty treats from kind people. He has his own resting pad, a donated woollen blanket and a waterproof coat. Sometimes Eve, John and Benjamin give me more than the price of a magazine and after work we go for a chocolate in the local café. I have the occasional flutter on the horses but have given up fruit machines. Six weeks ago I spoke to Angela on the telephone, she is at the same address and has a new manfriend.

We were able to laugh and teasingly I said "D'you miss me?"

EARTHED

Six months ago Carol had passed her driving test. Recently she had acquired her first car, a second hand Ford Fiesta. She had driven out alone a couple of times and once with her new friend Gemma. She planned to drive to her family on Sunday to show her parents and brother her new acquisition. Tonight was Friday and she couldn't wait to go out after a busy week at work.

"Hi Carol, what time will you be over?" said Gemma.

"About seven forty. I'm allowing half an hour to get there and I don't really want to be first there."

"I'm taking my heels with me."

"Good idea, I'll see you soon."

Rain was pattering on the window as Carol put on her skintight pink dress, bangles and bracelets and made the final touches to her make-up. It was January 17th, the day of Tracey's eighteenth birthday party. Carol, Gemma and Tracey all worked at an animal hospital in Great Charlbury six miles from Carol and Gemma's home village. Tracey lived in Great Charlbury itself, a large village in a valley flanked by wooded hills to the east and the floodplain of the River Awre to the west.

Carol, Gemma and Tracey were all vegetarians and wore cruelty-free make-up. The party was open to meat eaters but the food would be vegetarian.

The rain had eased when Carol trotted out to her little car. She checked her handbag for all the necessities and in five minutes there was Gemma waving at her wearing a large smile, a blue boob tube, under her coat, and a white skirt. Gemma hopped into the car gracefully and they set off.

"Your hair looks great Carol, did Melanie cut it for you?"

"Thanks. Yes, my sister's good to me, so's my brother Mark, he's a policeman."

"My brother's a builder, he's nice enough but he drinks too much."

"While we're on the subject, I know you don't drink Gemma. Would you mind driving us back tonight, I might have a drink or two?"

"That's if we come back together," Gemma chuckled. "Yeh, that's fine."

As they descended through the skeletal woods into Great Charlbury, the disc of the gibbous moon slipped out from the breaking clouds and the temperature dropped palpably. Carol turned into the village hall car park and manoeuvred cautiously into one of two empty spaces.

"Look's like it's warmed up quickly," said Carol.

"Yeh, we might be a bit late."

They slipped into their high heels and cavorted to the village hall steps.

"I wonder whether Susan's here? How does anyone disabled get in?" said Gemma.

"Over there, the ramp to the side entrance, silly," said Carol.

The cacophony of music and babbling assuaged them as they entered through the steamy glazed doors. Carol did some sharp mental arithmetic, fifty people, may be more. Tracey noticed them almost immediately and bustled her way politely through the throng and offered Carol and Gemma a genuine bear hug.

"So glad you could make it, can I get you a drink?"

"A mineral water, uh, sparkling for me," said Gemma.

"Martini and lemonade for me," said Carol.

Carol and Gemma found the only remaining empty seats rather too close to the Hi-Fi for intelligible conversation and shouted their hellos to Susan and to several people they knew. The sound system blasted *Temptation* by Heaven 17, ice clinked in Carol's glass and the room began to pulsate with the rhythm, light and stomping feet. It grew colder outside under the watch of the stars, the windows streamed with condensation.

"Hey David, shall we ask those two girls for a dance?"

"You're on."

Brian approached Carol and David Gemma and they took to the floor. David Bowie's *Let's Dance* boomed through the speakers. A bundle of balloons ascended and floated around the room and were tapped, pummelled and popped by the happy partygoers.

Party poppers exploded in the four corners. While dancing with David, Gemma caught Brian's eye lasciviously and for the next dance she joined Brian and Carol danced with David. Carol was slightly repulsed by the smell of cigarettes and alcohol on David's breath and after one dance they sat and talked uneasily. Brian and Gemma continued dancing, enraptured, becoming more amorous by the minute, as the musical tempo lulled to more romantic tones.

Eventually Brian and Gemma returned to some quieter seating and held hands while Tracey's mother called the room to order for the blowing out of candles, the cutting of cake and three cheers for her daughter. David offered to fetch Carol a drink but she rose herself and jostled through the crowd carrying another Martini and lemonade back to her seat. David stood and crept away sensing a little animosity. He approached another woman on the far side of the room for a dance as the music recommenced.

Carol stayed in her seat observing the scene. The floor had become tacky with spilt beer and perspiration. Undeterred, Brian and Gemma took to the floor again smiling graciously into each other's eyes. Carol became a little agitated and wobbled her way through the throng with another Martini and lemonade, noticing that Gemma had kept to her word and not consumed a drop of alcohol. Carol felt a tinge of jealousy mixed with sisterly happiness for her exuberant friend.

*

The clock ticked round to eleven thirty and Susan left via the side entrance and ramp. Mist billowed into the room as the doors were opened, the ramp a little slippery under the ghostly moonlight. Carol remained in her chair, pensive, her eyes fixed in the distance as eventually the D.J. called the last dance. A man in formal dress approached her for a dance and she accepted asking his name politely. "Kevin," he replied. Brian and Gemma were already strutting their stuff, locked in an embrace until the music fell.

The raucous laughter and merriment subsided as people began to drift home. Cold air met the alcohol outside to result in staggering and nausea in the car park. Tracey and her family made moves to collect up plates, cutlery, cocktail sticks and glasses whilst Brian and Gemma were deep in animated conversation in one corner of the room. Having said goodnight to Kevin, Carol looked at her watch, wrapped her handbag around her shoulder defiantly and marched over to them.

"Hurry up you two, I've got work tomorrow."

"Give over, Carol. I haven't drunk a drop and we've had a great time haven't we Brian." Brian nodded.

"I'm going out to the car. I'll see you there."

"O.K."

Carol wandered out into the midnight air. She felt a little giddy and she could see her breath. The earlier puddles were glazed with ice. Her windscreen was iced over. With growing exasperation she fiddled the key into the driver's door and groped around for her windscreen scraper in the door compartment. She was just making her first attack at the ice, when Brian and Gemma appeared at the doorway of the hall. Out of the corner of her eye Carol could spy them facing each other with arms around each other's waists in the milky lamplight of the thickening freezing fog. As she scraped fervidly at the glass, their lips conjoined in a passionate goodnight kiss. Carol had noticed them exchanging phone numbers in the hall.

*

Just as Carol completed a neat de-icing operation of which she was mildly proud, there was a dull thud and an agonised scream. Carol looked round in horror as Gemma was left in an ungainly sprawl of arms and legs at the bottom of the hall steps, writhing in pain. Brian, who had been a little over enthusiastic in his parting embrace had toppled her over on to the icy second step where, in her heels, her ankle had wrenched and contorted, buckling under her. Carol rushed over towards the stricken Gemma, in her heels, only to slip on a frozen puddle and land plumb on her backside shaken but unhurt.

"I'm so sorry. Are you all right? Can you stand on it?" said Brian, genuinely mortified.

Carol righted herself. Gemma began to sob loudly and tried unsuccessfully to stand on two feet. She screamed with pain as it became evident to Carol and Brian that she could not bear weight on her injured ankle.

"I'll call an ambulance," said Brian rustling through his coat pocket for his mobile phone. "Do you need a lift home, Carol isn't it?"

"I need my car for work today. I'm gonna have to drive home."

Brian called for an ambulance as Tracey emerged from the hall.

"We think she's broken her ankle," said Brian. "I've just called for an ambulance."

The shroud of freezing fog thickened and swirled across the face of the moon as Brian and Carol crouched and comforted Gemma. Streaks of make-up and tears etched her face as her sobbing became more muted.

"It's agony." she managed. "Honestly, I haven't had a drop to drink."

"We know love," said Carol trying to empathise with her best friend while contemplating an awkward drive home.

"I'll follow the ambulance to the hospital, if you want to get home," added Brian, brightly.

"That's very good of you, I ought to really," replied Carol, warming to Brian's concern and initiative.

The ambulance arrived through the turbulent fog. The ambulance crew worked efficiently and Gemma was stretchered to safety. There was a previously unnoticed gash on her left elbow that needed cleaning and dressing.

"Leave your mobile on as long as possible when you arrive. I'll be in to visit tomorrow, Gemma," were Carol's parting words.

Brian followed the ambulance out of the car park. Carol changed tensely into her driving shoes. She gathered herself as she turned the ignition. At least all seemed to be in working order in her little car. She endeavoured to focus as she left the hall car park nervously. There was an eerie hush around the village broken by the single peal of a clock bell. The contrast with the earlier bedlam was stark. The fog hugged the river valley like an undisturbed duvet. It was a proverbial pea-souper. Carol noticed having to blink repeatedly to keep her drowsy, glazed eyes alert to danger.

She progressed through the traffic lights at little more than twenty m.p.h. and began to climb into the wooded hills outside Great Charlbury. A rabbit darted across her path and she swerved to avoid it successfully but overcompensated slightly with her leftward swerve and struggled to regain control and avoid the verge. She drove onward out through the ceiling of the fog into bright moonlight but icy, untreated roads.

Carol wasn't clearly aware that she was travelling in loose zigzag uphill at about thirty m.p.h. She reached a road junction at the top of the hill struggling to stay awake.

She took off to the left cautiously knowing she was little more than two kilometres from home. Her attempts to concentrate were so great that she failed to notice bright lights in her rear-view mirror for a few seconds. Then she heard the blast of the siren and she pulled to an abrupt stop behind a police patrol car. She sat battling to hold back tears as two policemen approached from the police car. One of them tapped at the driver's window and she opened it resignedly.

"We noticed madam ... Carol!"

"Mark!"

Carol slumped forward still gripping the steering wheel. She must tell her brother everything, exactly.

FEAR NOT

Dwayne and Molly Fischer emerged from the chapel at Wild Salmon, Washington State arm in arm and were greeted with a warm handshake by the rotund and jovial Pastor Jim Forde. Several of the congregation stood in threes and fours outside on an unseasonably cool and grey June day chatting and laughing as swathes of mist topped the Cascades like woolly blankets. This was a church without a huge laity but their enthusiasm and piety made up for it completely. Dwayne and Molly attended every Sunday at 10am rain or shine during the spring and summer. In winter they retreated to their apartment in Portland to escape the worst of the snow and ice.

In years gone by they would have walked to and from the church but the return journey ascended steeply having crossed the river. Much to her irritation Molly's angina prevented her from accomplishing the walk these days.

In former days Dwayne would point out useful plants for herbal remedies growing by the roadside, usually missing some on the downhill walk but picking them out on the slower ascent home. Dwayne was a state-wide expert on herbal remedies.

Nowadays Dwayne's pick-up would grind up the hill in second gear, occasionally in first, until they reached their log cabin at the edge of the forest.

"There's still a lot of dew today," remarked Molly as they reached the front yard.

"Yes, the sun won't be scorching the herbs today. I think I'll cut some before lunch. I'll try to be back for one."

"Take Wilbur with you Dwayne. I've noticed he's been eating more lately, he needs the exercise. There'll be some gorgeous scents for him today."

Dwayne helped Molly from the passenger seat and they stepped into the spacious airy kitchen with its range and red and white floor tiles.

"I'll try and get dinner ready for one," said Molly pouring herself a glass of filtered water in order to take her medication. It baulked Dwayne a little that she had to take them, when he had a doctorate in herbal medicine, but he was still able to supply pick-me-ups to his family and friends particularly their daughter Jennifer, who lived in Wild Salmon.

Wilbur the brown Labrador bounded into the kitchen and jumped up to Dwayne's knees. He was two years old and full of energy. He had cost the couple $900 from kennels but had repaid them with boundless loyalty and fun.

"Alright boy, we're going in a tick."

Dwayne set his sights first on the cornflower in the back garden, which was blooming profusely. The back garden was large and untidy to the untrained eye, but for Dwayne it was a treasure trove of infusions, potions and lotions. As Wilbur sniffed happily here and there, Dwayne nipped some cornflower. Good for my dyspepsia he thought, an excellent all round tonic. He spotted a humble dandelion and thought of Mikey's insomnia and gout. Mrs Ward had trouble digesting fat and he recalled dandelion's stimulus of bile production in the liver. He would cut some evening primrose for more of his female customers and friends later in the day.

"Come on Wil, let's go into the forest, see what we can find."

Dwayne and Wilbur passed through the wooden gate which led to the path into the mixed deciduous and coniferous forest. Before they reached the trees Dwayne stopped at the miracle cure-all plant comfrey with its bright blue flowers. He knew that by July its medicinal properties would be severely limited as it died back. He also wanted some comfrey to enrich his compost heap. Dwayne had overheard Molly and Jennifer discussing Jenny's heavy periods, so he gave her a small vial of powdered comfrey to infuse every month. He wasn't sure whether she had realised from the frequency of his donation that he knew, but she told him that she had three cups of comfrey tea each month and felt fine on it.

Wilbur led the way into the forest, little sticks snapping under his paws, a thousand sweet smells to whet his appetite. Much of the undergrowth was still damp from the early morning fog and it was eerily dark for a summer noon. They had walked about 200 metres into the stand when Dwayne noticed a bright light in his peripheral vision accompanied by a growing whooshing sound. Wilbur barked loudly. At first Dwayne thought that the sun had appeared suddenly from the clouds but at the centre of the flash an apparition appeared descending quickly towards him. At this point Wilbur whined loudly and shot off into the undergrowth …

"Wil!"

The apparition settled not two metres away from Dwayne and Dwayne was petrified. The figure was dressed in pale yellow with large translucent wings and a white aura, with a darker yellow halo. The angel fixed his eyes on Dwayne.

"Fear not, Dwayne Fischer," he said.

"I am an angel of your almighty God, you have found favour with the Almighty."

Dwayne's jaw dropped and he began trembling.

"You have been chosen for a great mission at the Savar Health Centre, Chittagong, Bangladesh as a herbal therapist. You are to go for six months, God will repay your faith."

As quickly as he had appeared, the angel of the Lord disappeared through the tree tops and back into the clouds.

Dwayne dropped his rucksack; for fully five minutes he was rooted to the spot. Birds twittered but he did not hear them. His breathing was shallowed and accelerated, his fingers felt numb and his scalp was tingling. He felt a pressing urge to pass water. Eventually he turned his head and whistled shrilly for Wilbur, but there was no sign of him.

At this moment Dwayne did not feel like going to find Wilbur but wanted to amble home and ponder on the angel's message. As Dwayne left the forest there was still no sign of Wilbur but that was the least of a pious man's worries at present. Languidly he removed his boots by the kitchen step and crept into the kitchen.

"You're back early, love," said Molly turning to face him with a steaming pot of soup. She placed the pot on the side and studied his face.

"You look pale, is everything O.K.? No Wilbur."

Dwayne stood in silence for a few moments and avoided her gaze.

"Some idiots let off some guns in the forest and Wilbur legged it," he lied.

"Funny, I didn't hear anything love. Why didn't you go and find Wilbur?"

Dwayne sighed.

"He'll come back Moll, he's a clever beast."

"I hope you're right Dwayne, your hands are shaking, are you sure you're alright?"

"Yes I'm fine, the gunshots made me jump."

At lunch Dwayne picked over his food and the perceptive Molly didn't miss a trick.

"Wilbur's not back yet, were these bums real close?"

"Yes. If you don't mind I might go and see Jim Forde this afternoon, there's something I want to ask him."

"What's that on a Sunday afternoon?" Molly raised her eyebrows.

"I'll tell you when I get back love … if Jennifer phones tell her I'll call back later."

"Can you wait until Wilbur comes back, I don't fancy being here alone without him?"

"O.K, I'll ring Jim now in the study."

Fifteen minutes later after Dwayne had furtively found his passport and helped Molly with the dishes in an awkward silence, there was the sound of whining and scratching at the door.

"You're back, thank the Lord," said Molly relief stretching her face. Wilbur loped in and went straight to his basket ignoring his dinner.

"My you've had a fright," said Molly surveying the pair of them.

Dwayne drove down to Jim's cautiously. Things felt surreal and he was deeply perturbed.

"Hello Dwayne, you are lucky to see me at this time on a Sunday. How can I help you?"

"Can we sit in your study Jim? Something amazing has happened."

Jim raised his eyebrows and looked curious. They retired to Pastor Forde's study and Dwayne recounted the appearance of the angel. Pastor Forde took a deep breath.

"It's not unknown Dwayne and of course there were lots of occurences in Scripture."

"Problem is, I don't think I can tell Molly yet. It will be too much for her heart and she will worry herself sick, but I want to obey God's call."

"We can contact the Savar Centre for you on-line and explain, a six month stay could be arranged."

"But they don't even speak English in Bangladesh, Jim," said Dwayne handing the pastor his passport.

"There are many English there now Dwayne, Morris Nash went there five years ago. I believe he's still there."

"But who's going to look after Molly, Jim, she'll never manage on her own."

"Could Jennifer be persuaded, she has no children yet and she has transport?"

"This is beginning to sound very selfish Jim, causing problems for family."

"Leave the details of travel and accommodation with me Dwayne. I can ask other members of the congregation if they could help and even talk to Jennifer."

"No. Her husband is an atheist. I don't think he'll buy it."

"Relax and let our ministry team sort it all out. You have told me that you want to answer God's call, that's fair enough. After all the angel said only six months."

"There's another problem; we're due to return to Portland end of October. I may have to make it three months. What can I get done in three months?"

"Sorry, that had slipped my mind, but I'm sure the Bangladeshis will be flexible. As I said leave it with me for now. I shall not tell anyone about the angel's visitation before plans are finalised. We'll sort something out for Molly and you."

"Thanks Jim," said Dwayne rising shakily from his chair.

They shook hands.

As Dwayne returned to his pick-up the wind had strengthened, it felt cold and a few drops of rain had splattered his windscreen as he turned the ignition key. Dwayne wasted no time getting back to Molly.

"Ah there you are, Jennifer did phone, she's not too well herself," said Molly as he walked into the kitchen with a very pensive expression.

"You know you don't look right, love. Shall we have a redbush tea?"

"Camomile please Molly. I'm just going through to the study, won't be a minute."

"You don't want to spend any time with me today."

"I shall soon, just give me a minute, love," said Dwayne absently.

Dwayne hurried into his small study and dialled his daughter's number.

"Hello."

"Jenny, something incredible happened this morning; I saw an angel in the forest this morning who asked me to work at a health centre in Bangladesh for six months."

"Yes mum said you had been acting strangely, are you sure you weren't hallucinating?"

"Quite sure Jen. The trouble is I'm to go for six months as I said. I can't leave Molly alone in the cabin. Plus we're due back in Portland in the fall. I wondered whether you could find time to look after her while I'm away."

"That's asking a lot Dad, I'm two months pregnant and I'll have to ask Martin. I don't think he'll be that pleased, work's that hectic now."

"Jim Forde is right on side for me going and is setting things up."

"O.K, but I can't guarantee anything. Six months is a long time and I shall have to have scans and tests soon. I'll let you know."

That evening at supper Dwayne again picked at his food. He was usually a hearty eater.

"Still not got your appetite, love?"

"My stomach hurts a bit."

"I'll get you a ginger tea then."

Wilbur stirred from his basket, whined softly and did something unusual. He padded over to the table and placed his paw on Dwayne's knee, whining again quietly his big brown eyes staring into Dwayne's with a primeval gaze that Dwayne found quite comforting. Molly returned with two red mugs of ginger tea and a treat for Wilbur, which he chewed up gratefully.

Dwayne noticed her tremor and her pallid cheeks.

"Looks like Wilbur knows there's something up," quipped Molly.

A vehicle screeched to a halt outside immediately followed by a loud banging at the door. Dwayne was stirred quickly from his reverie to answer it.

"Hi Martin."

"Hi what?" said Martin striding across the threshold uninvited. "What's this cotton boll story about you seeing an angel? Have you been drinking too many of those bloody potions?"

"I did see one Martin."

"You've got a cheek asking Jenny to look after Molly. What do you think you're playing at?"

"To look after me?" said Molly, her face ashen and transfixed on Dwayne.

"Listen Martin, I did see an angel and I'm a Christian and I want to obey God's call."

"Bullshit."

"It's not …"

The argument stopped abruptly as both men turned their heads to the sound of a crash of wood on tiles. Molly had passed out and lay crumpled in a heap by the table leg.

"Oh dear God!"

"Now look what's happened, you bloody fool."

"Never mind that. I'll stay with her, you call an ambulance."

Dutifully, Martin dialled 911 banging the kitchen phone hard and irritatedly.

Dwayne placed his left hand gently under Molly's head and stroked her cheek with his right.

"Moll can you hear me?" He was aware of a large pink lump growing on her crown.

"I can hear you," whispered Molly faintly.

"We've called an ambulance, you're gonna be O.K."

Wilbur whined loudly and curled up in his basket.

Satisfied that Molly was conscious, Dwayne picked up her slight frame and carried her into the lounge. He placed her down carefully on the sofa, propping her head with cushions and then covering her with a blanket from their bedroom. The air was damp and cool, rain peppered the window. Dwayne lit the Calor Gas fire and sat down in the armchair, his head in his hands. Martin entered having calmed down a little.

"I've got to get going now, Jen has just called me on her mobile, she's vomiting a lot."

"O.K. thanks for phoning Martin."

Dwayne heard the slam of a car door and a vehicle rev up and speed down the hill.

As it was, Molly did not need to go to hospital after the medical staff attended her. She had been mildly concussed and they prescribed rest and recuperation. She came round completely soon after they left. She opened her lightly lidded eyes.

"What's this about an angel?" she said slowly and deliberately.

"I did see an angel Molly, it's not rubbish like Martin thinks. The angel told me to obey God's call and go to a Health Centre in Bangladesh to practice my herbalism for six months. I'm worried about you though, who is going to look after you while I'm gone? Also, are customs going to let me take American herbs into a foreign country? I'll need innoculations too. Jim hasn't told the church about the angel yet, though he's sorting things out with the Bangladeshis."

"He should tell the good people," said Molly. "Surely two or three of the congregation would be able to care for me ... Dirk, Frances, Geraldine."

"Yes possibly, but you would be here when it snows because we can't go to Portland, love. All this is stretching my faith, Moll I'm gonna be praying for us night and day."

"You go love, I'll be alright."

"I don't think you will."

Four days later, as warmth and sunshine returned outside, an oppressive gloom had descended on Dwayne despite snippets of encouragement from a less frail Molly. It was 11 am and Dwayne sat hunched in his study head in his hands. After taking Wilbur out that morning, but avoiding the forest, he noticed that the dog had been acting strangely. Wilbur would not eat up his food and had been whining in the night when Dwayne could not sleep. Also, Wilbur had been keeping closely to heel when walking with his tail tucked between his legs almost in sympathy with Dwayne's mood.

Dwayne's faith was surely being tested to the limit and he was at a loss to know what to do. He stirred and rifled through the extensive range of herbal remedies in the safe once he had unlocked it with trembling hands. Sweat dampened his brow and his stomach churned. Outside the eerie mournful call of bird exacerbated his desperation. Admittedly Molly was a little better be he still felt at the end of his tether. He picked out vials one by one but dropped three on the floor as his hands shook. He stooped to pick them up and was overcome by a wave of nausea. His hand alighted on a bottle of powdered belladonna and he just managed to unscrew the cap. He tipped a measure in his glass and fumbled over his secret supply of sloe gin in drawer of his desk. He poured a large measure into the glass with the belladonna but splashed some on the desktop. Desperately he pulled a handkerchief from his trouser pocket to mop it up when the study phone rang shrilly. At first Dwayne did not want to answer it, but a picture of frail ill Molly, alone and grieving flashed across his mind and he thought he heard a whisper in his head saying; "You're a good man Dwayne, don't hurt Molly."

"Hello," he muttered into the phone.

"Dwayne it's Jim, you sound a bit unwell."

"Yes ... I suppose so."

"Good news my friend. Had an e-mail this morning from the Savar Health Centre in Bangladesh. You can go with Molly, there will be clean, air conditioned accommodation for both of you. Also the authorities will allow you to take your American herbal remedies. You will be working with a local herbalist to garner a supply of local herbal remedies as well. We sorted your visa, you just need to book your flights from Seattle. They would like you to go away from the main rainy season October to March. You need to see your doctor and nurse for your jabs."

"Thank God for you Jim ... and all your team. I'll be down to see you after Molly comes in with Wilbur."

Dwayne collapsed with relief in his study chair.

Just then Molly walked in with Wilbur who bounded in wagging his tail.

FIRED EARTH

As the sun's disc rose shining primrose instead of orange, the people returned from their ceremony at dawn. Arga, one of the millers, had stayed behind to clean and prepare his quern. The precious grain was stored in earthenware jars with lids tight enough to exclude most of the damp. Arga's partner Hyda, who had made the jars, was brewing nettle tea on a trivet over a wood fire, the beads of her necklace hanging over her full bosom. The fire spat and popped cheerfully. As a small posse of onlookers carrying pails and buckets from the spring gathered at the barn door, Arga and his son Marc turned the grinding stones and broke into raucous song. The bystanders joined in chorus for a while before scurrying to their huts to make breakfast.

By noon Arga and Marc had ground jars of grain and were exhausted. They sat to chat over a rustic beer, the froth from which clung to their beards and moustaches. Having sieved it carefully, Hyda had been putting the freshly ground flour into jars. By now people were straggling back from the fields in threes and fours, weary from work in the warm sunshine and in need of sustenance. Some limped, some stooped, some of the elders were hunchbacked. They talked softly, some laughed. The more infirm had stayed behind in their circular huts spinning wool and repairing clothes.

Arga mixed spring water into the priceless flour in a metal bowl, steadily and thoughtfully. His muscular arms contracted and relaxed with the rhythm of the stirring. He was making sourdough using the yeast in the air to raise the dough as it stood in the barn after mixing.

That afternoon Arga, Hyda and Marc took their turn in the fields, harvesting and stooking. After threshing, some of the poorer grain was taken to the pigsty by Arga for the hogs to gobble up gratefully. At sunset the weary threesome returned happy in the expectation of baking bread despite the rashes and bites on their sandalled feet. Arga went to inspect his dough but for the first time ever it had vanished.

Arga racked his brains. With two millers at the hill fort, why would anyone want to steal the sourdough when not baked? The people all received dry flour. The last thing a community whose lives depended on co-operation needed was petty pilfering. He exited the barn and turned to Hyda who was rubbing comfrey leaves on to her ankles.

"The sourdough's gone."

Hyda had been trying to conceal the fact that she knew that Blanca had been making eyes at Arga for a little while. Yesterday morning Hyda had noticed that Blanca had stayed behind from the dawn ceremony on the pretext of caring for her sick daughter.

Hyda knew that Blanca's daughter was indeed poorly, but at the door of her hut whilst stirring her porridge Blanca's focus was at the longbarn entrance where Arga and Marc were preparing the quern. Hyda was sure that Arga was far too preoccupied to notice Blanca's scrutiny. Blanca was widowed now, her partner had died of a chest problem. He had threshed the barley for many years and had inhaled its mould laden dust.

Hyda was quite demure and had not challenged Blanca with her suspicions for the sake of group harmony, but Arga had noticed that Hyda was not leaving his side to attend the new potter's wheel as often as she was accustomed.

"Perhaps a wolf took it," offered Hyda.

"Nonsense, there would have been a mess."

"Perhaps Jon will know where it is," said Hyda speculatively, trying hard to appease. Jon was the other miller who lived at the hill-fort, but whose barn was a good third of a mile away near the northern perimeter ditch. Arga's mill was near the southern perimeter ditch.

"I'll go and see him I suppose," said Arga grumpily.

The evening was calm as Arga set off to see Jon. There was an ubiquitous aroma of cooking and bread baking as the fires blazed in the waning light. As Arga approached the other mill he could see Jon at the fireside sharpening a blade with aplomb. Jon's partner Hannah was slicing vegetables into a blackened pot half-filled with bubbling water. Arga came straight to the point.

"Some of my sourdough went missing this afternoon while we were at the fields."

"I don't think I can help you," replied Jon laconically.

"We can't tolerate stealing here. If we do, we will die and retribution will mean that we'll die anyway."

"We may need a camp meeting," offered Jon sagely.

"Can we spare the time with harvesting going on?"

"I'm sure if the community is to survive we can meet."

The next morning Arga went to the dawn ceremony. He intended to address the majority of the people there and then. Marc was left to clean and prepare the quern.

Hyda accompanied Arga to the circle, Blanca was absent apparently to care for her daughter. When flags were laid down at the end of the ceremony, Arga moved to the centre to everyone's surprise. He told the assembly about the theft.

"It may seem minor but it is of grave importance because, as you know, if disputes break out our community is lost."

There was a murmuring through the crowd, nodding and shaking of heads. The mood was subdued as people filed back to their huts.

When Arga rounded the corner of the barn he noticed Blanca talking to Marc near the quern. Arga was irritated and his eyes bore into the pair of them.

"I thought you were caring for Anna, not wasting my son's time with chatter."

"I was asking Marc whether he would be able to remove Anna's tooth. It's hurting her so much."

"Isn't Jana better at that kind of thing, she removed two of mine."

"Maybe ask Jana," said Marc kindly as Blanca eyed Arga and Hyda warily.

"Perhaps I shall," said the nervous Blanca and darted back to her hut.

Arga frowned at Marc. The sourdough incident was beginning to make a noble and discerning man quite paranoid.

"What else were you talking about to Blanca?"

"Nothing in particular," said Marc defensively.

"We can't afford to waste time," snapped Arga glancing up at the gathering clouds.

"I'm going to the potting hut. It looks like rain," interjected Hyda emboldened to leave Arga after his stern rebuke of Blanca. She scuttled away.

"You haven't turned the quern," Arga challenged Marc.

"No, Ruben's not well, he couldn't help me."

"Come on, let's get started."

As the rain lashed down Arga and Marc rotated the quern but in silence today as Arga's mood was still disagreeable. At the potting hut Hyda moulded the clay dextrously into bowls and jars. She was by far the best potter in the settlement but she had a nagging worry about Blanca's intentions that overshadowed her concentration.

Nevertheless, with great resolve she threw two pots and a jar during the morning. At about noon Jana hurried into the potting hut in some distress. Hyda turned and stopped the wheel.

"Ruben's really ill, he won't eat. I've just come from Blanca's, I removed Anna's bad tooth, she screamed her head off."

"I heard," said Hyda softly. Hyda cleaned the wheel, washed her hands and replaced Jana's sodden shawl with her own. She curled a comforting arm around Jana's emaciated shoulders. The rain eased sufficiently for them to light a fire with dry tinder from the hut. Hyda pulled a wrapped bag of crushed rosehips from her pocket. She believed it would make a soothing tea for stressful times. She brewed it in a bowl over the potting hut trivet. When Jana calmed down a little Hyda asked Jana of Blanca's whereabouts.

"As far as I know she is mending her daughter's clothes while Anna rests on her bed," said Jana flatly. Hyda looked across to the barn. Arga and Marc were sitting supping beer as was their wont at noon.

"She hasn't been to the barn?"

"Why do you ask?"

Hyda breathed in deeply. She would have to reveal her secret thoughts.

"I suspect her of stealing the sourdough."

"Blanca. Really," said Jana looking into the fire. "Why would she steal it? We all get our ration."

"She's jealous of Arga and I. She has no partner."

"I don't think she would steal but I suppose it's possible now you mention it," replied Jana still staring into the fire.

The next day a second batch of sourdough disappeared from the barn despite Arga placing it less conspicuously. When Arga returned from the fields with Hyda and Marc he was enraged. Hyda felt it was time to broach her suspicions to her partner as she had observed his moodiness over the last few days.

Without more ado Arga stormed over to Blanca's hut, but Blanca was not there, only her daughter lain on her bed breathing shallowly. He decided not to disturb the sick child. His next thought was to search the settlement for her but he pondered a little and decided to hatch a plan to catch the thief. He stepped briskly back to Hyda who was preparing supper. He stood over her for a while and then announced, "Perhaps you could go to the fields tomorrow with Marc and I could lie in wait for the thief in the barn."

"They would notice you're missing. You're such a conspicuous member of the community," replied Hyda softly.

"You could say I've had to attend the pigs."

"The pigsty is visible from one of the fields," said Hyda.

"Maybe you could tell them I am poorly and have to rest."

"Alright dear, that may not be far from the truth and we need to put a stop to this nonsense."

Arga went to bed that night feeling slightly less irritated. At least he had his partner's assent. Hyda was quietly pleased but warned him not to be violent with any intruder.

The next day Blanca's daughter Anna died. There was not enough firewood available for a pyre so the elders and Blanca decided to bury her. Virtually everyone from the settlement attended the burial, apart that is for Arga and a few of the very infirm like Ruben. People noticed that Arga was missing and began to mutter about disloyalty, having been addressed the previous week in such an uncompromising fashion. Hyda felt anxious. People like Hannah started asking her awkward questions. She stuck close to Marc. Also she felt unable to offer Blanca condolences with her suspicions lurking in the back of her mind. Eventually fright got the better of her and many heads turned as she left Marc bemused and sprinted back to the barn.

"I should never have gone," she gasped to Arga on arrival. "They're getting irritated about you not being at the burial. They could turn on us."

That afternoon Arga stayed defiantly at the barn. Hyda told the workers he was ill and with a great deal of tact she managed to persuade them, but she did not feel comfortable even with Marc beside her.

Arga crouched in the dark corner of the barn nearest the door. There was thick dust and masses of cobwebs and bird droppings to avoid. It was a thoroughly boring wait but he was determined. He tried hard not to fidget and to keep his normally loud breathing, quiet. His pulse rate increased and beads of sweat dotted his dirty brow.

Arga's joints were aching and he was about to give up his vigil, when quiet as a mouse someone entered the barn door. Arga could just see a shadow at first. The intruder crept forward eyeing the prominently placed pitcher of sourdough. Arga was vaguely aware of shouting people in the direction of the fields as he darted out and grabbed the intruder around her slender waist as she picked up the pitcher. Then in the gloom he recognised her stricken face. Jana!

"But I've run out of flour and Ruben won't eat."

GOING UNDERGOUND

The day had dawned clearly at the campsite, but cumulus clouds had developed slowly as the campers went about their preparations in a leisurely fashion. By 10 am it was sticky and the midges were biting under the canopy of trees as Justin, Monique, Daniel and Carla ascended the steep path from the pasture below. The entrance opened before them forbidding and mysterious near the summit of the hill.

The adventurers stepped into the gloom with their head-torches glowing brightly. Within forty metres the air was palpably cooler and clammy. The passage walls were damp but all four students were focussed on their footing; the irregular rocks jutting up into floor, glistening with moisture were a trap for the unwary.

“I hope this doesn’t go on too far,” said Carla.

“Don’t worry we have plenty of time, I told Mrs Wiseman we would be back before four,” said Daniel in a reassuring tone.

Justin led the group followed by Monique both of whom had experience of potholing. For Daniel and Carla it was an inaugural adventure.

After ten minutes the passage floor was smoother walking and it began to descend. After a sharp left turn the passage opened up to reveal a large cavern.

“Something interesting here,” shouted Justin back to the others.

Soon all of them were standing in a huge cave with a pool at its base fed and drained by a trickling underground stream. The headtorches revealed impressive ranks of stalactites, some dripping metronomically into the pool, some dripping down the cavern walls making calcite ropes.

“Wow!” said Carla her voice echoing around the chamber as the four of them gazed in awe.

Large stalagmites grew in the far corner of the cave. The cavers listened silently, for a minute or two, to the sound of water trickling and plopping. Justin broke the silence.

"I hope the flash will be bright enough," he said undoing the Velcro on his bag. Daniel was carrying the white coiled line so that they could retrace their steps. He was a photography student.

"Should be with the torch light," he said producing a large camera with a zoom lens from his back pack. The students stayed in the cavern for what seemed like ten minutes but was nearer half an hour, flash light ricocheting intermittently off the calcite.

"Shall we follow the stream down there," said Monique eventually. "There might be more to see."

Justin looked at his watch.

"Could do, we've plenty of time."

"But you don't know how far it goes," said Carla nervously.

"We can always turn back, we've got the line," said Daniel.

"Yes, but what if it gets snagged on the rocks and breaks?"

"It shouldn't do love, it's plastic coated."

"Let's get going," Justin said impatiently.

The four exited the cavern heading gently downwards in a rocky passage, Their boots splashed in the little stream at its base. They were forced to stoop at times as the ceiling lowered. Carla now clutched the line, her heart pounding.

After 150 metres or so they encountered a problem. The passage narrowed and was only a metre high from top to base.

"I wonder how long this is?" said Justin. "We're going to get wet."

All of them were wearing showerproof jackets.

"I told you we should have gone back," said Carla.

"Don't keep moaning," said Justin curtly.

"Tell you what, I'll give it a try, if one of you can carry my knapsack a minute," said Daniel.

Daniel was closer to Carla than Monique and Justin and wanted badly to allay her fears. He snaked his way into the passage which had a slight bend to the right. A few minutes of crawling later, he called back.

"It's O.K. It's not far. Looks like it opens out into something big."

"Great, I thought we'd find something spectacular," enthused Monique, putting on her waterproof trousers.

"I'd better keep these cameras dry too," said Justin stuffing his camera into Daniel's rucksack.

"I'm going to get my underwear wet," said Carla.

"I can't wait," joked Justin.

All four of them slithered along on their hands and knees, their bellies occasionally dipping into the flow. Carla was again not sure she could go much further; the cold water made her feel nauseous and she felt scared despite unravelling the white line. Monique followed Daniel boldly and was soon catching him up. Justin brought up the rear, the rucksack brushing and bumping against the rock ceiling despite the smoothing of the passage floor by eons of erosion. Cheekily he patted Carla's bottom.

"Stop that," she blurted.

"Only a bit of fun, you're doing fine," said Justin.

Ten minutes later Daniel reached the passage end with Monique on his heels. He squawked with delight as he viewed a cavern the size of at least a small cinema fall away in front of him.

Monique glimpsed it too and said, "Come on Carla, this is amazing."

"It better be," said Carla. "I'm soaked."

To the left of the entrance were three stepped ledges just wide enough to clamber but to the right there was a vertical precipice to the abyss below.

"Come on it's worth it," called back Daniel. The sound of water cascading from the small stream echoed around the cavern. One by one the potholers emerged on the narrow first ledge, Justin having to balance precariously carrying his and Daniel's luggage. Carla was holding the line with one hand and the top of the ledge with the other. There was just enough room for them to dangle their legs over the first ledge before the precipice. Carla was uneasy again . . .

"How long do these torch batteries last?" she said to Justin who was carefully unpacking Daniel's and his own smaller digital camera.

"Ages I think, try not to worry."

Carla looked at her watch. Amazingly they had taken two and a half hours since leaving the campsite.

Gazing upwards Monique could see a display of stalactites high above her, not nearly as grand as in the previous cave but awe inspiring nevertheless. Daniel leaned forward as far as he dared. His headlamp revealed another large pond into and out of which the rivulet flowed. He hauled himself back and began taking flash photographs of waterfall to his right. Justin was also snapping happily but realised that the torchlight may be insufficient in a cave so large and dark. He consulted Daniel and Daniel replied it was just best to try to snap the waterfall as he had.

Monique, a vegan, opened her lunchbox. Inside was a container of red pepper houmous, salad, brown rolls and fresh pretzels. She nibbled a pretzel and dipped into the houmous.

"Good idea," said Carla who opened hers. Ham and tomato sandwiches, a bag of ready salted crisps and a yoghurt.

The two women munched happily but Carla's clothes were still damp and she shivered. Justin and Daniel packed up their cameras and joined them on the upper ledge.

Despite the clammy chill, the four were contented with lunch and transfixed by the beauty of the scene. It was Carla who was first to sense danger. She tapped Daniel's shoulder urgently.

"Daniel, the flow's getting stronger, shouldn't we be getting back now?"

Daniel, who had been munching chocolate raisins, looked to the passageway. The flow was indeed getting rapidly stronger.

"Justin, pack up quick," he shouted. "We could get trapped."

"Hold on to that line for now," retorted the usually calm and authorative Justin.

Within five minutes the water flow had risen to a torrent. Carla began to sob loudly.

"I . . . I told you we should have gone back."

"We'll have to wait a while, it's probably a flash flood," shouted Justin trying desperately to keep calm.

"I'll leave my headlamp on, you others conserve your batteries," said the quick thinking Monique.

The four of them sat stunned by the deafening noise of the water, now half way up the passage walls. With one head torch on it was extremely dark and frightening.

The next hour seemed like an eternity. Carla hugged Daniel close to her, stricken with fear and trembling. Daniel shivered. For once in their lives Justin and Monique were dumbstruck. Still the cacophonous torrent of water issued from the passage and Daniel was scarcely able to hold Carla and the safety line simultaneously.

"Justin could you take the line?" he bellowed above the din.

Justin shuffled over and grabbed the line urgently without speaking.

"At least we told Mrs Wiseman that we were coming to the caves," said Monique trying to raise gloomy spirits. "Maybe she will raise the alarm if we're here much longer."

"It's only five past two at the moment. Could be just a bad thunderstorm," said Justin.

Carla was still terrified and becoming very cold but said nothing in the security of Daniel's arms. He felt little better taking responsibility mentally for his foolhardiness. Monique racked her brains to find some distraction from the predicament that assailed them. Then spontaneously she began to sing. *I Shall Be Released* echoed sonorously around the chamber. Justin, who had never held anyone's hand since his childhood, grasped Monique's and joined in. Their combined voices just about drowned out the sound of the slightly receding water. The effect was enough to rouse Carla and Daniel who added their voices to the chorus.

Monique began to bellow at the top of her voice and Justin wished he could record the tumultuous acoustics for posterity. The four sang for fully twenty minutes before they became hoarse. Daniel told a few of his favourite jokes he'd picked up at college and played paper, dynamite, rock with Carla obligingly lit by Monique's headlamp. Gradually the flood water began to recede.

"We'll get out of here yet," said Justin.

Back at the inundated campsite there was consternation on the face of Mrs Wiseman. There were four tents on site; two of them were being used by the absent students. They had collapsed under the force of the rain. The other two were occupied by the Johnson family, who were baling out their groundsheets. It was a miserable sight for Doreen Wiseman, she had never seen lightning and rain like it in her sixty-nine years and she feared for the safety of the students who hadn't returned. It was now 4.10pm.

The hot sun had reappeared and was raising fumaroles of

vapour from the tents and grass alike. Mrs Wiseman scampered inside and pressed 999 for Fire and Ambulance. The operator told her that the road from Elmsley was partially flooded and coming through were numerous flood related calls. Mrs Wiseman explained the situation as calmly as she could. The caves were a good kilometre up and away from the campsite and it would take the emergency services at least twenty-five minutes to reach the hamlet of Southwood.

In the cave Carla, in her damp clothes was beginning to feel the effects of hypothermia. Daniel, Justin and Monique huddled around her trying hard to keep Carla and themselves warm. Monique's headlamp had dimmed and Justin had switched his on. The flow in the passage had dropped to about 15cm deep; but it was doubtful that Carla could crawl back through without worsening her condition and Justin realised that.

"We'll get out alive chums," said Justin.

"Yes," said Daniel and Monique in unison.

Carla said nothing.

JOB

It was May. As I reached Job's front door I noticed the coal shed to my right was nearly empty. Next to it stood the outside toilet with the peeling paint on the door and old fashioned pull latch. Behind me Job's two Jersey cows chewed languidly at the long, lush grass in the Church field. A handcut beech thumbstick was propped against the wall next to the door. I knocked softly as not to be intrusive. As was his wont, Job called "hello" before he stepped slowly towards the door. He beckoned me in with his artisan's hand now gnarled with arthritis and smiled across his weather-beaten ruddy complexion.

A metal pail of milk covered with a red-checkered tea towel stood at the larder entrance. On the simple, robust square table was placed a loaf of bread on a solid breadboard with a large knife; a half-drunk mug of tea, a small dish of butter, a wedge of cheddar cheese and half an onion. On the draining board stood a bowl of soapy water along with a bar of soap, a flannel and a small shaving brush.

Job wore his red neckerchief and hat as usual. As the little electric bar-heater slowly warmed the chilly kitchen, Job needed little prompting to recall times when he ploughed with horses. Nineteen twenty-one had been such a hot dry summer, but nineteen twenty-two nearly washed out the harvest. There were bucolic stories to fill a whole evening. I listened intently.

(This extract is based on a real acquaintance, set in the 1980s. He has since gone to the Lord.)

JOY, DIFFIDENCE AND DESPAIR

Joy has bright red hair and sparkling emerald eyes. You can see the hair stretching out gaily in the summer breeze as Joy rides a bicycle through the park. Joy has the smile of an impoverished child receiving a beautifully wrapped Christmas present. The skin on Joy's face is soft, unblemished with rosy red cheeks, her chin is strong but still bares humility. Light dances through every strand of hair creating a spectrum of rich wild auburn. Joy moves rapidly and unrestrained without melancholy or introspection but is receptive of others who feel her joy. She wants to participate in the simple pleasures money cannot buy. Joy emanates from Joy's being into the whole cosmos and every living being needs to know how Joy feels.

Diffidence has a hunched back and shuffles along in worn-out slippers. It wears grey and looks around the next corner with an anxious expression. It taps at obstacles with a knobbly stick and rarely raises its head to acknowledge a passer-by. Yet basically it is pure of heart without conceit and is innocent of the impression it gives. It sits at the back, wants to trouble no-one. At the party it slips off quietly to bed with its book, curls up between the sheets and sleeps snugly.

Despair has black tear stained sunken eyes with reddened cornea, a pitted skull, black oily hair and an ashen face. Its face is barely visible under a black hooded cloak under which is spiky heavy chainmail. Despair talks to no man as it steps laboriously along the wet paving slabs with its head bowed. It has a pitiless bonecrushing mood of utter loneliness and gains no solace from others' platitudes of hope. It relates little to others as it believes no other can comprehend its predicament. It is on a wet, dark road to nowhere and is best kept off four wheels.

K.D. JONES

Keith Jones waved cheerily to Jim Hoskins the platform manager and climbed into the driver's compartment of the 1540 from London to Glasgow. He always liked to dress smartly in his West Coast Mainline uniform. His black shoes were clean and his hair cut neatly. He kept his A.S.L.E.F. membership card in his inside jacket pocket and his handkerchief tucked into his outside breast pocket. A bottle of mineral water was held at his side from which he would sip while at stations and red signals.

For a bachelor, Keith was quite fastidious about hygiene and tidiness and a slightly anxious disposition hadn't stopped him from completing twenty years as a train driver. He had many acquaintances among railway staff and one very close friend Peter, whom he met at the Labour Club in Leyland, when on leave. Before this latest journey he had been chatting contentedly to railway staff at Euston. Keith had the comfort of knowing that he would drive as far as Preston where Bob Granger would take over the second leg of the journey. Keith had met Bob before at staff change overs and they were quite amicable.

Keith departed Euston on time and the eight coach train carrying 187 passengers trundled through the metropolis and North London suburbs. As the crepuscular light gradually began to fade Keith accelerated into the Buckinghamshire countryside. A pall of cloud advanced from the west blotting the crescent moon to a milky sliver, while the eastern horizon remained crisp and starlit.

As the train approached Nuneaton travelling at 80 miles per hour, Keith noticed a figure hanging down from a bridge as far away as his headlights would illuminate.

Suddenly, the figure dropped in a heap on the rails before him. Startled, Keith jammed on the brakes as hard as he could without derailing the train. But too late, the train screeched to a halt as the sprawl of arms and legs were mutilated by the wheels.

Keith was stunned and began to tremble as he reached for his mobile phone.

"Hello, yes. There has been a fatality on the West Coast Mainline just east of Nuneaton we need help urgently," he rattled.

The emergency services had to park on the bridge from which the victim had jumped. They sealed off the road to traffic, temporarily, before they could remove the victim's remains for identification and to inform relatives. One of the ambulance crew approached Keith who had stumbled out the driver's compartment shaking visibly.

"Are you O.K?"

"Not really. First time in twenty years. We'll have to get another driver out here, I don't think I can ... carry on."

Keith could feel his chest tightening and his pulse accelerating.

"We'll take you to Nuneaton Hospital as a precaution, you may be suffering from shock."

Two rescue staff guided Keith down towards the bridge. Keith meandered as gravel crunched underfoot. The three of them clambered up the embankment by a narrow path to the safety of the bridge. From there he was whisked away to hospital behind the ambulance carrying the dead victim. The ambulance crew's observations confirmed the worst, Keith's blood pressure was low, his pulse rapid and thready, his skin clammy.

Keith took several seconds to orientate himself when he awoke the next morning. He gleaned that an intravenous infusion supplied his arm, but everything seemed unreal as if in a dream. Later, a nurse offered him a light breakfast but all he could manage was a glass of cold water.

Thirty-six hours later Keith's vital observations had returned to normal and the staff had arranged for Peter to pick him up and take him home to Leyland. Keith was stony silent during the journey and gazed straight ahead into oblivion. At first Peter tried to converse but decided to concentrate on his driving and turn off into Keele Services to see whether he could coax a few words there. Duly, they arrived at the service area and Peter guided Keith through the busy concourse.

At the table they sipped bottled water because tea and coffee were expensive. Eventually after much prompting Keith said, "It's just I feel so guilty ending a young bloke's life."

"It's not your fault, Keith, you did your job well."

"What about his family? How are they going to feel? I'm still alive. I would have liked to go to the funeral."

"Would that have been appropriate? You never know someone feeling very emotional could have become irate with you and really it was not your fault. Why don't you and I go for a round of golf on Wednesday, the forecast is good."

"Sod golf. I want to get my head straight first."

"Keith, I know you're still in shock and it may be a bit … premature to ask, but are you thinking of going back to the railways?"

"No, probably not … I was thinking in hospital perhaps I need to take my life in a new direction that heals the hurt."

"Like what? Any ideas yet?"

"I'm not sure yet. Come round on about Thursday if you like, I mean if you've got time, and we can chat about it."

Peter felt they had made tentative steps towards Keith's rehabilitation and Peter was not at all concerned that Keith remained silent for the rest of the homeward journey.

Peter dropped off his friend at his flat as the sun set on Sunday afternoon.

"Give me a bell if you feel grotty."

"I shall, thanks Pete."

Keith added that he would go to the Labour Club next week as he would like just to chat to his friend and anyone from A.S.L.E.F. who might be able to help.

Keith sat for hours and hours in front of the television that evening without really absorbing or concentrating on anything. It was all just a babble. It seemed incongruous for an apparently tough train driver to shed tears but small rivulets slipped down his cold face. He sighed and struggled to lift himself from the chair, yawned loudly and shuffled to his bedroom.

Keith lay awake for hours now the solitude and his thoughts met so indecently. The metronomic ticking of his alarm clock tortured him. Several times he got up and stepped somnambulently down the stairs to his little kitchen, to pour himself a drink.

The last time this happened it was 3am.

The next thing Keith knew was his phone ringing. He woke with a start and looked at the clock. It was 12 noon. Keith roused himself as quickly as possible.

It was Will Thompson from A.S.L.E.F. Northwest Region.

"Hello Keith do you mind if I come over, see how you are and what we're able to do for you."

"Alright Will, but I warn you I'm still a bit dazed by it all."

"Tomorrow morning then?"

"Make it 2.30, it seems I'm gonna have trouble getting up."

"O.K. See you then."

Keith spent another evening of torpor after managing to buy groceries that afternoon.

However, he was getting more irritated by his own indolence and perhaps, though he might not be consciously aware of it, that was the sign that action was required.

Nevertheless when Will arrived he was in a rather resigned mood.

"As you have paid your membership for twenty years we can offer you sick benefit for at least six months on top of your statutory sick pay."

"That's good of you but I shall probably look for a different job, do some training."

"After your sick pay runs out you may be entitled to Job Seeker's Allowance. We all wish you well in whatever path you choose."

"Thanks Will."

*

Keith had always cooked for himself on his days off, partly to avoid wasting money on expensive take-aways and partly because of his aforementioned fastidious nature and mostly because he liked discovering new dishes. He decided to start cookery classes at college and mentioned it to Peter when he visited Keith on Thursday. Peter was actually concerned, in a sexist sort of way that Keith was becoming emasculated.

Peter had noticed also that some bins with large labels CARDBOARD, PLASTIC, PAPER had appeared in the hallway. Sagely, Peter kept his concerns to himself, for any positive move in whatever direction Keith wanted seemed a good idea.

Keith persevered with his cookery and in two years achieved NVQ Level 3. He was enjoying happier times and met Hilary through attending a Ramblers club. Their friendship had blossomed gradually. When his sick pay and Union Benefit had expired Keith managed to find a part-time job as a kitchen assistant in a café in Leyland, while he furthered his qualifications. Keith started cycling again, a hobby he had previously enjoyed before his work moved him around the country. Peter and Hilary cycled with him on alternate Saturdays. They all found the expansion of The National Cycle Network with traffic-free routes very tranquil especially for Keith's nerves.

Keith recycles most of his refuse now, makes regular donations to Friends of the Earth, and has had his flat fully insulated. In the early days of his difficulties he received many messages of support from his friends in the railway industry. Bob visited three times during the six months after the incident.

Keith ascertained that another driver was found for 187 stricken passengers and they did arrive in Glasgow albeit two hours late. This news eased some of the guilt that surfaces in Keith's mind still.

Hilary stays alternate Friday nights and Keith travels to hers by bus or by bicycle (if the Lancashire weather is fine). Keith has an independent spirit now and has one great ambition to be the chef on the Greenpeace ship, *Esperanza*. Not even Hilary is going to stand in his way.

MIZAKE THE MIZAN

(for Elizabeth, Robin and Simon)

Mizake the Mizan was to inspect his fiefdom. As he emerged from his luxury wooden palace, the reverent and not so reverent waved mauve and white flags that wrinkled and flapped in the dawn calm. Mizake had a shock of auburn hair, a long pointed beard and wore a brown woollen hat. Conch shells dangled from his ears and numerous bangles clinked about his wrists. He sported a red tartan waistcoat and knee length brown boots.

As Mizake strode out into the chilly air his eyes stern and fixed, the lowest caste elves ignited hundreds of fireworks which blazed through the sky with a cacophony of explosions and subtle hues of azure, green, pink and primrose. Far behind the palace dozens of fallow deer cavorted in fright.

The light blue silk of the hot air balloon billowed in response to the flaring of the burner like a fast growing giant mushroom. The bottom of the basket was obscured by an ethereal mist. It was secured down ready for take-off by nymphs and elves holding fluorescent guy ropes. "Let it be done," bawled Mizake with flaring nostrils, as he marched forward, loyal flag bearers at his side.

Shenzin the Mizani had high cheek bones and a white porcelain face radiating serenity and peace as she stood patiently in one corner of the monstrous wickerwork basket, just her head and shoulders visible to the assembly. Mizake growled under his breath as he hauled himself into the basket with less grace than a beast. Shenzin kissed his stubbly cheek lightly and he held her in a crushing bear hug as the elves released the restraining ropes. The burner fired hoarsely. The balloon rose out of the dewy glade and over the forest. Everyone below – people, elves, Mizake devotees – could see impending disaster as an intermediate elf called Josiah was suspended on a guy rope from the rising basket, squealing desperately for help. Mizake and Shenzin were either oblivious or ignorant of his predicament. As the burner roared they were locked in a passionate embrace. With a despairing cry Josiah's grasp loosened and in the eyes of the throng of onlookers he whistled down to annihilation in the forest canopy, his guy rope flickering in the low sunlight.

Mizake gazed over the unfolding landscape of his fiefdom. Down below, little ant-like people and elves scuttled in and out of the glades and villages. To his right the rising sun made the rocks glow in rich ochres and oranges. All this was his: lakes, rivers, plains and forest. Wherever he and Shenzin chose to land there would be willing help to ground them from their devoted subjects.

Back in the capital the crowd stared aghast at Josiah's plight. There began howling and wailing from the elves. The people cried, for Josiah was much loved. What a horrid spectacle for Mizan's subjects to witness. Gradually the mood of the people became more mutinous. As the balloon floated away into the far distance, cat calls of "Down with Mizake," rose up. There was muttering of dissent and shaking of heads. The ire of the elves was set like never before. The crowd surged forward towards the palace veranda upon which stood Tenyatta the Zabor with his arms outspread to address the crowd.

"Let us not rebel. Mizake is a great and noble leader. Josiah's death was just a terrible accident."

But the response of the throng was unanimous. Cries of "Death to Mizake," rose as mauve and white flags were ripped, torn and shredded.

Elves squealed to a crescendo. Tenyatta once again tried to appease their wrath.

"People of Mizana, we have no replacement for Mizake, he is our salvation."

People of all ages flooded into the palace tearing at the timbers with their bare hands.

Some hurried to their huts to gather tools of destruction, tinderboxes and anything vaguely flammable. Tenyatta panicked, clambered down from the veranda and ran for his life. The Mizanas chopped, sawed and hacked through the palace as the flames crackled and belching black smoke plumed above. "Death to Mizake, Death to Mizake," rang out between coughing and spluttering. The charred palace was soon unrecognisable.

Mizake and Shenzin had landed their balloon softly and skilfully near the goblin village of Urs. Having received the oblations and fervour of the goblins, Mizake and Shenzin were fixed up with a horse drawn carriage which the goblins kept for special occasions. Mizake and Shenzin set forth on the ground level return journey pulled by two snow white horses and Myag, a goblin driver at the reins. "We shall visit again soon and thank you," Shenzin told the goblins.

Mizake and Shenzin chatted gaily waving to onlookers as the carriage wound through the forest on dusty dirt roads, colourful fungi decorating the woodland floor. Hot but dappled sunlight illuminated the flowers in every shade along the way. Lianas twisted around the ancient trunks of oaks and planes.

The idyll was interrupted by a high-pitched wailing coming from a tall ash tree. Shenzin nudged Mizake and he asked the driver to halt the horses. There dangling high in the tree was Josiah, sobbing loudly attached to his fluorescent rope.

"Please climb the tree and try and rescue him," said Shenzin softly to Myag. The goblin shinned up the tree trunk to the first branch with deceptive agility. Soon Josiah's wailing stopped as his rescuer approached. Myag slung the slight Josiah on to his back and carried him piggy-back down the tree. "A great effort," boomed Mizake as a rabbit scuttled by, disturbed by the commotion. "Put him in the carriage," said Shenzin. "And make him comfortable."

Josiah stayed snuggled in the foetal position all the way home. He was thankful and did not make a sound. On arrival at the edge of the glade that delineated the capital, the carriage was met by a large angry crowd. Shenzin turned her head in fear but Mizake rose and tried to appease the people and elves. A hail of eggs and gourds peppered the carriage. One gourd hit Mizake square on the ear and the conch shell pulled his ear painfully. Myag squealed for mercy being the only goblin, but it was Mizake that was the focus of their wrath. "Josiah, Josiah, we love Josiah," they bayed as Mizake, with glazed eyes, watched wisps of black smoke billowing from the smouldering remains of his palace. The crowd was gathered now around the carriage.

Bravely, Mizake rose to address them and Shenzin stood and grasped his hand.

"Josiah is alive, I can show you him." The hub-bub subsided a little, many jaws dropped as Mizake himself helped Josiah out of the carriage and carried him up to front seat for all to see. Slowly, the crowd ebbed away, silenced and in fear of retribution.

So began an age of austerity in Mizana. However, elves received greater rights and there was more freedom bestowed on the people. Mizake and Shenzin had a new, more modest dwelling built and conducted themselves with compassion and dignity.

The new shoots of an egalitarian Mizana had sprung.

NAKYMUNI

The autumn breeze was a reviving shock. Lisa had persuaded Nakymuni to walk with her to the allotment garden and maybe help her a little if Nakymuni wanted.

"You can sit and watch if you want," said Lisa brightly as she faced Nakymuni in the doorway of her flat.

"What is there to sit on up there?"

"There's an old wooden fold up I use when I have my flask or when I just want to watch the bees," explained Lisa. "I'm sure if it carries me it'll carry you."

Yes Muni had lost a lot of weight. Thank goodness for Lisa, she had been such a good friend all the time Muni had been on chemotherapy and when she had been first diagnosed. You see all her living relatives were in Japan now. Being so poorly she hadn't been over for eighteen months. They could scarcely afford to visit her either.

Lisa was an old work colleague at the bank before she moved on to administration, she was a little more bouncy and extroverted than Muni. Muni was more the thoughtful type. They complemented each other well. Muni could fill her in on the details while Lisa made the running.

This was the first time out for a distance for Nakymuni and she was worried that the wind would loosen her wig. Her knees cracked and her ankles grated like she was the Tin Man in the *Wizard of Oz.* Lisa kept to a sedate pace.

The allotment was quite sheltered but the soughing of the breeze in a long stand of conifers was quite audible. You could almost taste the freshness of the Arctic air as the chrysanthemums stood defiantly erect in Lisa's flower bed. There were a few weather-beaten dahlias in reds and pinks and striking violet asters. Large orange pumpkins sat plumply on the damp soil. Nakymuni kept her hat and gloves firmly on, while Lisa rummaged in her tool shed and emerged carrying her luxurious spongy kneeler and a trowel that had seen years of faithful service.

"I'll do a bit of weeding and maybe you can help me sow some garlic."

Muni didn't know much about garlic but was very willing to learn.

While Lisa weeded, Muni explored the well-kept patch. There was a herb garden. Muni rubbed the leaves of the lemon balm between her long thin fingers. The evocative tangy odour as she raised her hand was very satisfying and went to the primitive corner of her brain. There was thyme, rosemary and the last stand of lavender before the winter frost.

On the next Monday Nakymuni worked on the allotment with Lisa and on the following Saturday, when it was unusually mild, they planted some over-wintering onions. Eventually as her demeanour improved and with a little persuasion from Lisa, Nakymuni set off for the allotment alone with the keys jangling in her trouser pocket. You see she was determined to learn more. That afternoon Lisa had gone to visit her son in Walthamstow but not before giving Muni a piece of paper with her mobile phone number on it. She had also given Muni strict instructions not to do more than thirty minutes' forking, but Muni was sorely tempted to do more such was her emergent enthusiasm. However, on inspection of the amount of work ahead common sense prevailed.

Two other tenants were working on adjacent plots. She guessed their age to be slightly older than hers. She recognised them from previous visits but didn't know their names. To her left a man was digging. He was fairly short and stocky and the sun reflected from his bald head. He was wearing a check shirt and a pair of beige trousers that seemed a little too big for him. He had a strong fleshy Caucasian nose and a little grey stubble around his chin. Muni approached cautiously.

"Hello," she said nervously. "I'm Muni. With your experience could you tell me if it's the right time for forking?"

"Could be," he replied gruffly not looking up. "But the frost should break it up."

"What's your name?"

"Eddie." Still concentrating on digging.

"I'm Nakymuni."

"Oh."

"You have a nice garden. Have you worked it for many years?"

"A few."

The next day was showery. Nakymuni wore her light anorak, as it was quite mild, and her blue wellington boots which laced at the front.

The evening before she had recounted to Lisa her time on the allotment with great gusto over a mug of redbush tea. Lisa liked fruit and herbal teas and was only too glad to share.

"In the summer, I sometimes make my own infusions," she explained happily. "It's the last job to pluck the leaves before coming home because the leaves wilt so easily.

"By the way my brother is coming about 4.30, Friday afternoon, if you would like to meet him. He's very practical, he's a carpenter."

"I really would like to meet him," said with her typically Japanese good manners. But Lisa could tell she meant it.

"Good. Do you want the allotment keys for tomorrow? The day after maybe I can come with you in the afternoon."

"If you would be so kind, I'm really enjoying it. What would you like done tomorrow?"

"Perhaps you could trim back the woody herbs, like the lavender and thyme."

Nakymuni was not alone on the allotments today either. Eddie was back filling his composter with pumpkin leaves. On the plot to her right, mulching his soil with compost, was a tall gaunt man with fair hair and prominent cheek bones who was whistling softly. She hoped he was more communicative than Eddie.

"Hello, I'm Nakymuni, do you mind me asking what you are doing?"

"I'm mulching my soil," said the man. "I'm Graham by the way." He seemed quite sociable thought Muni.

"What is mulching please?"

"I use no-dig methods to grow my crops. It involves mulching the fertile upper layers of the soil and letting the worms and bugs take it downwards without damaging the soil structure. I have to get lots of compost delivered from the mushroom growers. Luckily I can afford it. I grow shallow rooted crops like these lettuce and endive, radish in spring, onions, strawberries and raspberries in summer."

Nakymuni nodded trying to make good sense of what he was saying.

"No-diggers believe that the spade damages the fertility of the soil by bringing less fertile subsoil to the surface."

"Eddie does a lot of digging," offered Nakymuni.

"Well each to their own but I prefer no-dig and what's more it's easier on your back when your older."

"Thank you for answering my question, Graham, I hope I see you again soon."

"You're welcome, rain coming I reckon."

Nakymuni trimmed back some overgrown lavender meticulously for a few minutes, musing whether to approach Eddie for his view on things. From the corner of her eye she could see him digging fervently. She wandered off to him trying to look inconspicuous and reverent.

"Hello Eddie."

"You again." He carried on digging.

"I wanted to know whether I could compost these lavender trimmings."

"Course not."

"Graham might."

"No 'e wouldn't they're too woody." At last he turned to face her, right foot on top of his spade blade.

"We don't have an incinerator."

"Well get one."

"Do you think I could grow some cuttings?"

Eddie sighed deeply.

"Didn't we fight you nips in the war?"

Nakymuni was quite taken aback by the racist overtones.

"Clear off and talk to that pansy, Richards."

"You mean Graham?"

"That's right," said Eddie, his face flushed as he began to dig furiously.

"I come down 'ere for a bit of peace, not to have nips badgering me."

Nakymuni scarpered back to Lisa's allotment quite shocked and a little scared. Was this man going to set on her? She noticed that Graham had slipped off home. A chill shiver went down her back as the first spots of tuppenny sized rain splattered her anorak. As she sought shelter in Lisa's shed her hands grappled with her mobile phone. There was no reply so she left a quick message for Lisa on the voicemail.

For a short time the rain was torrential. Muni wanted to go to Lisa's tout-suite as Eddie was stomping down the road which passed Lisa's shed carrying his spade over his shoulder muttering something about the bloody weather. Yikes he could hit her with it. Nakymuni decided to run to the allotment gates and on to Lisa's house but her aching limbs in the aftermath of her chemotherapy restricted her to a gentle trot.

As the rain eased she fumbled for her gate key, she must keep as big a distance between her and Eddie as possible. As a gesture of appeasement she left the gate open for Eddie who was obviously heading the same way. Luckily Eddie seemed preoccupied with his thoughts and didn't quicken his pace.

With the breeze freshening and the sky brightening behind the cold front, Muni scampered down the lane and took a right turn into Brook Street which led to Lincoln Avenue where Lisa lived at number 24. At the corner four youths on bicycles were talking loudly with voices berating each other with expletives. Nakymuni kept her head bowed, eyes glued to the pavement. But this made her all the more conspicuous and vulnerable as the youths sized her up. They followed her on their bicycles as she vainly increased her pace. They began to hurl abuse and threw their cigarette ends at her.

"Please leave me alone, I'm a sick woman," she offered bravely. One of the youths who appeared to be the ring leader picked up a stone and was about to throw it at Muni, when there was the sound of a stern woman's voice from behind them all.

"Jack Davis put that stone down!" Nakymuni glanced back briefly as she strode on briskly. She assumed that it was Jack Davis's mother issuing the order. The four boys shrank away sullenly back down the street as Paula Davis stood there defiantly hands on hips eyes glued on their every movement.

Nakymuni was exhausted and at the point of collapse when she rang Lisa's doorbell. She sat down droopily on the doorstep the very moment that Lisa pulled up in her car.

"What on earth! Are you alright?" exclaimed Lisa jumping quickly from the car.

Whilst gasping for breath Nakymuni explained as best she could what had happened.

Finally, as they entered the house she said "I don't think I should go to the allotment on my own anymore, I was quite frightened."

"Have a cup of hot chocolate with me," replied Lisa apologetically. "If I knew that kind of thing was going to happen I wouldn't have let you go. It did seem a bit risky but you're so keen and you enjoy it. I must have a strong word with that Eddie when I see him. I think his father fought in Burma, that might have something to do with it."

"Surely that's all over now, Japan doesn't have an army."

Nakymuni spent a good three hours at Lisa's house. She couldn't believe how lucky she was to have a close friend in Britain now that her husband had been dead for five years.

Nakymuni had recovered markedly by Friday having seen the district nurse on Thursday, but Lisa insisted on picking her up to take her to meet Thomas rather than let her walk on her own.

"Hello, I'm Thomas." Nakymuni guessed the man's age to be

roughly the same as hers. She was drawn to his muscular tanned forearms and huge hands. He was average height with sandy coloured receding hair and a warm smile. His teeth shone white and immaculate, his nose broad and fleshy. He gave her a firm, friendly shake of the hand. Nakymuni warmed to him.

"I hear you have been helping on the allotment."

"Oh yes … Lisa hasn't told you then … I had some trouble last time I went."

Nakymuni explained what had happened.

"Sounds like this Eddie character needs sorting out."

"I don't want any fighting," pleaded Muni.

"There won't be any I suspect. You really like it up there don't you?"

"I did until this happened."

"Tell you what, I'm free on Sunday, maybe we could go up together or with Lisa."

"Yes. Lisa was telling me you are very practical," said Muni more positively.

"I'm a carpenter if that's what you mean?"

"I've a lot to learn, I'm interested in herbalism."

"Yes, Lisa likes that as well. I used to take lots of painkillers, but Lisa's herbs and the Herb Shop seemed to help with special exercises. Wouldn't expect that from a carpenter would you?"

They both laughed and the crowsfeet aside of their eyes showed mutual happiness.

Thomas caught the moment.

"Nakymuni would you like to come out to dinner tomorrow night? I know a nice place on the Springfield Road called Tardelli's. It caters for couples and is really cosy."

At that moment Lisa slipped by with a tray holding two pots of chamomile tea and three pieces of home-made carrot cake.

"You singles getting on O.K.?"

Nakymuni bit the bullet.

"Your brother has asked me out. Will you not get a bit jealous? I would think it would be quite natural, not to flatter myself."

"Not really Muni, I've just started dating a nice man and quietly I've been hoping that Tom would find a nice lady for ages!"

ONCE BITTEN TWICE

Margo felt the fresh cool of an early June morning on her rosy cheeks. The dawn chorus was settling as the low slanting sunlight illuminated the walls with coppers and ochres. The noise of light traffic was audible but not assuaging. Immediately he saw the lead, Margo's playful red setter Oscar had begun thumping his front paws on her thighs in expectation of his morning walk. Margo called him to heel and clipped the lead. She popped a tissue and a treat in her jacket pocket.

By the time Margo and Oscar had set off the sun was reflecting from windows of the two local tower blocks and offices and enriching the hues of the Victorian chimney pots. It was a five minute walk to the park but Margo always allowed ten because Oscar exploited the extendible lead to sniff at most of the lamp posts and discarded morsels as well as the seemingly uninteresting patches of grass.

Two men stood near the park entrance chatting. One with a short-haired German shepherd dog having rather groggy back legs, the other with a more docile and obedient greyhound.

"Good morning," offered the bearded man with the greyhound as Oscar strained the lead to the limit investigating the German shepherd. The dog growled menacingly and his owner, a short man with salt and pepper hair, tried to pull the dog to heel to no avail.

"Bruno!"

Bruno and Oscar snarled and growled at each other with Bruno in the ascendancy.

Margo bent forward to physically restrain Oscar by holding his collar while the man with the cap tried to restrain Bruno. Bruno lashed out and sunk his incisors into the back of Margo's left hand. Blood poured out. Between them the two men managed to wrestle Bruno to the ground just as he was about to nip Oscar's ear, as Oscar beat a hasty retreat towards Margo.

*

"I'm terribly sorry madam, my dog can be in a lot of pain from his hips. I don't usually muzzle him at this time in the morning."

"Well you should have, he nearly bit my hand off. It's a good job I've had a recent tetanus booster."

The back of Margo's hand had a deep ugly tear right down to the tendons, with stinging pain and oozing blood.

"Can I walk you to the hospital?" said the greyhound owner.

"He should really," said Margo gesturing angrily towards the German shepherd owner, who was beating a hasty retreat out of the park to retrieve a muzzle from home.

"I'm a playwright you know and I'm left-handed," said Margo irritably. "I may not be able to do any writing for weeks."

"Call me John. We'll go to Casualty shall we?"

Luckily, the hospital was little more than ten minutes walk away since Margo's hand throbbed with pain.

"I can't flex my hand," said Margo to the nurse as they arrived at Casualty. John left her with words of sympathy as he couldn't really enter A&E with his dog, however placid.

The nurse cleaned the wound and arranged some analgesia. The wound was deep enough to necessitate being packed with sterilised gauze with a large dressing attached over the top.

"I suppose I could type with my right hand, one or two fingers for a while, but I prefer to write longhand and edit while I type. Oh dear life seems so difficult, there's no sick pay for us freelancers."

"You might get sickness pay with a doctor's note," said Nurse Graham cheerfully. "I'll give you a pack of dressings, some sterilising solution and gauze," she continued.

"If it starts bleeding again come right back. I'd see your G.P. as soon as possible," she said while deftly making a wrist sling. Outside Oscar began to whine loudly.

Margo plodded home disconsolately and Oscar caught the mood, his tail staying resolutely between his legs.

Over the next few weeks Margo's wound healed quickly but slight tendon damage restricted her hand movement greatly. The skin, however, was taking a long time to heal and after two visits to her doctor's she was referred for a skin graft and possible plastic surgery at a reputable London clinic.

On the day of the appointment Margo decided to travel by tube as her hand was too painful to drive far. It was a grey, cool July morning when she departed, having put Oscar in the care of her obliging and pleasant elderly neighbour Mrs Lucas, for whom she ran errands regularly.

Margo descended nervously down into the tube station keeping her handbag clasped at her side. She preferred to queue at the ticket booth than use the machine. She could hear a jumble of Spanish and German being spoken by the people at the front of the queue. Eventually she obtained her ticket and walked watchfully towards the escalators down to the Northern Line. As she reached the platform she thought she recognised a man in a brown trilby hat, limping slightly. Moving forward she edged round him and looked into his eyes. The man started slightly.

"Uncle Kenneth!"

"Margo!"

"I didn't know you used the tube, Uncle Kenneth."

They entered the busy platform. The next train was due in four minutes.

"I don't use the car so much now, in any case it's in for its MOT today. Aunty Michelle is picking it up later," said Kenneth eyeing Margo's left hand.

"I'm going into St Thomas's skin clinic, they might do a skin graft on my hand soon."

"I was only going to the cinema and I haven't got a ticket. Perhaps I can accompany you," said Kenneth kindly.

"Oh that's very kind of you but there's really no need."

"I insist, that really looks a nasty injury."

"You might have a little wait while I'm there, it's a dog bite."

"I'll come with you, maybe you'd like to come back to ours for tea afterwards."

"That's so kind, although I won't be able to stay too long because Oscar's at Mrs Lucas's next door. But she does walk him when she's up to it, so maybe I can call back later." Margo rang Mrs Lucas and all was well. She said she would take Oscar for a walk.

The train rumbled into the station and the babble of voices was drowned by mechanical screeching. Margo and Kenneth managed to find the last available seats in a carriage. Both felt better for having company as the train rattled and entered the dark tunnel. They remained silent for a minute or two.

"Shall I ring Aunty Michelle to tell her we're coming, when we reach Tottenham Court Road?" suggested Margo brightly.

"Yes, good idea. She should have picked up the car by the time we get back. It's she who does most of the driving these days. I'll prepare some tea for you."

Uncle Kenneth had been a chef in a top London hotel in his younger days before he found the pace too much and made a complete change of direction becoming a civil servant at the Department of Trade and Industry. He had retired recently but remained quick witted and active despite a little knee trouble. Margo had always got on well with him, probably better than with her father who died of a stroke five years earlier.

Tottenham Court Road was not the nearest tube station to St Thomas's but Margo didn't want to change trains, so she and Kenneth took a taxi to the skin clinic for which she paid.

"Your mother well?" said Kenneth as they zipped through the bustling streets.

"As can be expected, Ken, I saw her at the weekend."

"We must visit soon, I'll phone tomorrow," said Kenneth feeling a tad guilty that he didn't see his sister-in-law as often as he should.

"Michelle is always so busy."

Michelle was five years younger than Kenneth and still worked part-time in a florists in Victoria. Kenneth and Michelle still adored each other and it was quite unusual for Kenneth to be out alone.

Margo and Kenneth had a twenty-minute wait at the clinic before Margo was called in. There were two other patients in the waiting room, a young man with visible burns to his face and another young man with his leg in plaster and ugly lesions to his exposed foot. Margo felt her fate to be lucky by comparison. The air was rather stuffy, quiet classical music played and a couple of vigorously growing rubber plants in the corners boughed under the spotlamps. Kenneth yawned loudly.

"Excuse me, it's quite hot in here."

Soon Margo was ushered into the surgery by a charming almost coquettish young woman who inspected the wound carefully. Despite the air of arrogance and aloofness she presented, Margo was touched by the compassion and concern the specialist showed her.

"We shall be able to offer you a skin graft for this area once the bruising subsides. I shall refer you to the dermatologist for treatment in about ten days if the bruising allows. You will receive a card in the post by then. If the wound starts oozing or becomes inflamed contact your G.P. and make an appointment with her immediately."

"Thank you."

Margo re-entered the waiting room to find Uncle Kenneth with his chin touching his chest snoring loudly. Margo caught a smile from the receptionist in her peripheral vision.

"Uncle Kenneth time to go."

"Oh! Uh!" Kenneth's head juddered and his neck straightened. His cheeks were flushed as he stretched out of the chair and flexed his dodgy knee.

"Must get my knee seen to soon, Margo. I was going to the cinema; that wouldn't have done it any good. Anyway let's go home for some tea."

"Good idea, take your time though," said Margo kindly.

Margo and Kenneth took a crowded bus to Wandsworth in bright, humid July sunshine. There was a group of raucous school children on the bus firing paper pellets from rubber bands before the bus driver stopped, strode down the gangway and chided them brusquely then stomped back to the wheel. Things quietened down.

The bus was less full for the second half of the journey and Uncle Kenneth who had been silent began to perk up, telling

Margo funny anecdotes from his days as a chef.

"Press the buzzer Margo would you, this is our stop."

They alighted on to the hot pavement. Heat seemed to radiate from everywhere; bricks, mortar and tarmac. Uncle Kenneth took off his trilby and mopped his brow with his handkerchief. Margo pulled out her mobile phone.

"Hello Aunty Michelle, it's Margo, we're quite near now."

"What's that rapscallion up to now. It's a good job I've collected the car or I wouldn't have been here to meet you … But it would be lovely to see you."

"Uncle Kenneth is going to cook us something."

"Well I hope we have the ingredients or he'll be going to the shop for them. I'm bushed what with the florists."

"Uncle Kenneth is as well, Auntie, he's over-dressed for the change in the weather."

Ken and Margo trudged through the streets back to the quiet avenue and up the steps to the couple's spacious two bedroom abode.

"It's been a while, how are you?"

"I was bitten by a dog and am unable to write lately."

"Oh you poor thing, come and have a drink with me."

Kenneth peeled off his layers, washed his hands and peered into the fridge.

"I could do Spanish omelette, chips and salad, would that do?"

"Sounds lovely to me," said Margo taking a hot cup of peppermint tea from Michelle.

"I don't know how you can drink that on a day like today," said Michelle reclining on the sofa opposite Margo, clinking the ice in her orange juice.

"I let it cool down, then it's great."

The mingled aromas of egg, pepper, tomato and onion wafted in from the kitchen while Kenneth whistled loudly. "Should be ready in fifteen minutes," shouted Ken gaily.

Margo and Michelle chatted happily about the extended family and then Michelle took Margo through to the newly renovated garden with patio, lawn and flower borders. The foxgloves were alive with bumblebees and other insects cut through the steamy city air around the women's heads. Margo flailed them away with her good hand. There was a rich display of colours on show with the taller plants at the back of the quintessential English herbaceous border.

"Ready!" called Kenneth.

The three of them retired to the cool, fresh dining room and tucked in.

"It's always cool in here. In winter we have a convector heater going," said Michelle.

The meal revived Kenneth to his usual jocular and humorous self and he spouted much convivial banter.

Margo noticed it was nearly eight o'clock.

"I must go and pick up Oscar now, thank you so much for having me."

"Pleasure," said Kenneth. "I'll drop you home."

"No Ken, I'll see to that," said Michelle. "You load the dish-washer and see to the cat."

Ken assented a little grumpily as he thought his wife was over-protective of him most of the time.

As she drove through Victoria towards Battersea Michelle said "Ken's not so spritely these days, I was worried when you first phoned. It was the first time he's been out without me for weeks."

"There was a little sweat on his brow but I don't think he's too bad really. I think he still loves you dearly, let him live," said Margo.

"You know maybe I am a little demanding, now you mention it."

Michelle dropped Margo off and Margo thanked her genuinely. Margo scuttled round to Mrs Lucas's immediately and rang the bell.

Mrs Lucas took a while to answer the door until Margo heard the soft padding of her slippers after Oscar's bark.

Mrs Lucas opened the door and Margo noticed immediately that her face was grey and troubled. Margo saw the dressing on Mrs Lucas's left hand.

"Oscar is fine … but a dog bit me through its muzzle when I was walking him. Had to have six stitches at the hospital."

PLACE MATS

Rosemary collected the place mats from her ample wooden sideboard. They were her best. Images of rose, carnation, azalea and delphinium adorned the centre, a frieze of campanula around the edges. She sighed, turned and placed them in a habitual manner opposite each other on the freshly laundered red tablecloth spread over the small oak dining table. She fetched sparkling clean cutlery from another drawer and bright clean wine glasses. As a little embellishment, white napkins were wedged into the glasses.

Perfect. Just as John would have liked it.

John and Rosemary disembarked from Flight 135 Qantas Airways at Melbourne that January morning. Squinting across the tarmac, while adjusting to the steely bright light they reached for their sunglasses. The day was pleasantly warm rather than stiflingly hot as they had expected.

Marlene was waiting at the check-in desk for them looking impatient, peering and shuffling her feet irritably. Perhaps they had been held up at the baggage conveyer, sometimes it took ages she mused. Marlene looked at her watch again shifting her weight from left foot to right as she grew more anxious. She was alone now, all the other passengers appeared to be reunited with their loved ones.

Marlene had married Tom in England five years ago and emigrated to Australia, last year, to fill two teaching posts in different schools. This was her parents' first visit.

Marlene approached the check-in staff, a woman with bleached blonde hair and manicured nails.

"Excuse me, my relatives have not come through to meet me. Can I go through to see what's happened?"

"Have you any form of identification?"

"No, but I'm getting worried about them."

"I'm afraid you cannot without ID madam."

"But I know they were on the plane. They phoned me from the tarmac at Heathrow."

"I'm afraid I'm not allowed to let you through. We can check the passenger list for that flight if you could hold on a moment."

John and Rosemary had just reached the terminal building when John felt a crushing around his ribs and sharp pains down his left arm. He stumbled and slumped down to his knees as his right hand dragged Rosemary sideways. In moments John was prostrate, gasping and crying out in pain. Rosemary shook while she reached for her mobile phone. The jittering of her hands made it difficult even to phone 999. It didn't occur to her that 999 might not be the right number in Australia. Out of the corner of her eye she spied a member of staff while John's crying abated and his eyes glazed.

"Excuse me! Excuse me! My husband has just collapsed."

A posse of onlookers had assembled but Marcus, the member of staff, dispersed them quickly and phoned for an ambulance.

"Paramedics will be here as soon as possible madam."

"Thank you."

"Could you bear left please and not congregate here," said Marcus to further curious onlookers.

Rosemary kneeled down and stroked John's face gently, his chest was rising intermittently. Still shaking, she placed her fingers on to his wrist. She couldn't feel a pulse but maybe that was because of the panic she felt herself. She stood up amidst the blare of announcements. The concourse was clearing between arrivals. She must phone Marlene.

"Hello, Marlene."

"This is Jessica Haynes, I think you have the wrong number."

Marlene paced around the arrivals gate and glared at the check-in staff.

"I can confirm that John and Rosemary Smith were booked on Flight 135 from London."

Marlene continued pacing back and forth, her fists resolutely jammed in her pockets.

"Thank you," she said with a false toothy smile. At that moment her mobile phone buzzed and played a familiar soothing tune. Marlene grabbed at it.

"Hello!"

"Marlene it's Rosemary. John's collapsed, he's barely conscious. I'll let you know which hospital they're taking him to, maybe we can meet up there. The paramedics haven't arrived yet."

"O.K. Rosemary, I'll wait for your call."

"Would you like to take a seat over there and someone can bring you a bottle of water," said the blonde haired check-in staff having heard Marlene's story.

"No thank you, I'll stay here until I get another call, all the same," said Marlene more kindly.

"The toilets are down there on the right."

"Thank you," said Marlene quietly, realising that the woman was only doing her job as efficiently as possible.

A queue of people began to form at the check-in desk. One or two glanced at Marlene.

She felt conspicuous and mildly paranoid. They seemed to have curious expressions.

Maybe it was the expression she had on her face that was provoking the odd look, she mused, trying to rationalise the paranoia.

The check-in staff worked efficiently directing people to the baggage depository, occasionally looking up to check on Marlene's welfare. After what seemed like an eternity, Marlene's phone rang.

"Hello Marlene, the paramedics are here. They've done some CPR and electric shock treatment. They say they're taking him to City Infirmary. How far away is that?"

"It's about twenty minutes drive for me once I've got out of the car park, I haven't rung Tom yet. I'll try and ring him at school when I get back to the car. I should be at the hospital in less than half an hour."

"Thomas."

"I've just come through the door, Mar, what is it?"

"John's collapsed at the airport. Do you want to come in to City Infirmary or sort things out there?"

"I'll come in."

"O.K. I'll be at Casualty."

Rosemary sat hunched up in the ambulance while the paramedics tried to revive John.

As she dabbed her sodden cheeks, they told her that they had some breathing and a pulse. An ethereal moment of life thought Rosemary, perhaps they'd get him back. If he did live they would need to reclaim their suitcases from the airport she thought in the matter of fact way one sometimes thinks when a crisis is taken out of one's hands.

As the ambulance swung into the Accident and Emergency bay, Rosemary could see that John's face had turned puce. His breathing was intermittent as the paramedics worked gallantly. Marlene and Thomas were waiting at the entrance after fast and hazardous journeys to the hospital.

"Oh Marlene and Thomas … so good to see you. I hope he pulls through," blubbered Rosemary through a veil of tears.

The Casualty staff were efficiency itself as John was wired up to cardiac monitor after another session of CPR. His relatives watched with gaping mouths.

"Hi, Marlene," a voice pierced the silence.

A man with his arm in a sling, sitting in the corner, turned Marlene and Thomas's heads. Rosemary was rapt with her husband.

"Oh hiya," offered Marlene in as casual a voice as she could manage.

"Who's he?" said Thomas glaring at his wife.

"Someone I know at work, don't worry," said Marlene avoiding her husband's gaze.

"Like who?"

"A relief teacher."

Tom inspected the stranger.

"Doesn't look the type to me."

"Well he is," said Marlene irritably. "Stop fussing, we're here for John."

*

"We're very sorry Mrs Collins but we have been unable to revive your husband."

Rosemary collapsed into a plastic chair, her head in her hands, sobbing loudly.

The next evening Marlene, Thomas and Rosemary were sitting in a pleasantly decorated modern restaurant in downtown Melbourne. Rosemary stared into space silently, occasionally looking at the place set at the table that would have been John's.

"I don't know how I'm going to cope with the flight home."

"That's three weeks away. We can still give you as good a time as possible till then," said Thomas.

"There will be a lot to sort out at home, I should go earlier."

"Why not spend some time with us, it's good to be with others when you're down," said Marlene.

"Not always, I'd really like to grieve alone, not cause you problems."

"There'll be plenty of time for that. See a bit of Australia with us, after all you haven't been before," said Thomas.

Rosemary reflected quietly then fiddled with her cutlery nervously as a waitress came to take their orders.

"Lovely place mats," she said softly to the waitress.

"Thank you madam."

Marlene, Thomas and Rosemary were half-way through their starters when Marlene's mobile phone played its distinctive tune.

"Hello."

"It's Aaron darling, I've bust my arm real bad. When are you over again?"

Marlene glanced at her husband. She would have to choose her words carefully here. "Not for two weeks at least, we have a bereaved visitor with us."

"But Mar, I'm in real trouble, it's my right arm."

"Well you'll have to manage it yourself."

Marlene hated herself for saying this but she was in no position to express her heart-felt compassion despite being totally bored with her husband.

"I'll try and manage. Love you."

"Take care, bye."

"Who was that?" said Thomas.

"One of my students wanting to see me about difficulties with an essay I set," blurted Marlene truly amazing herself at being so quick witted.

"I must remember to shut it off when I'm out."

"My students don't ring me," said Thomas. "Seems a bit odd to me."

"Yes but you're not teaching the same age group," said Marlene defiantly.

The three of them ate in silence for a while as Marlene regained her composure and Rosemary and Thomas struggled for something constructive to say.

During the main course Rosemary suddenly blurted: "I might kill myself in the aeroplane toilet."

Thomas winced. "We hope not."

"How would you do that exactly?"

"I've been on anti-depressants for a couple of months. I ... I don't like telling people but John and I had been having problems."

"Don't worry we won't ask what problems."

But Rosemary felt so desperate that she wanted to reveal all.

"We had problems in our love life."

"You don't have to tell us more."

"He was such a lovely man too," said Rosemary.

"Maybe in a couple of years you'll find someone else just as nice," said Marlene.

The waitress came back. Thomas ordered a glass of wine for Marlene and himself and a spritzer for Rosemary who didn't drink.

"Remember we're driving. Perhaps one of us should have a soft drink."

"Alright then. Three elderflower spritzers please," said Thomas irritably.

"Would you like desserts?"

"Lemon sorbet for me dear," said Rosemary.

"Chocolate brownie for me please," said Marlene.

"Fruit cocktail for me please," said Thomas. "I'm watching my weight," he said to Rosemary, while glaring at Marlene.

"Never does any good whatever you're watching," chuckled Marlene mockingly, longing for Aaron's light-hearted good humour.

"Now you two, you're worse than me," said Rosemary.

Marlene and Thomas showed Rosemary the scenery of Victoria under metallic blue skies and brilliant sunshine. From the western end of the Snowy Mountains through Bendigo to the Murray river. They travelled along the coast to The Ninety Mile Beach and The Lakes National Park. There was an uneasy truce between Thomas and Marlene for Rosemary's sake. Rosemary couldn't have been more grateful to them but was too preoccupied with grieving to notice much discord.

On February 7th there was a tearful farewell at the airport.

"Don't do anything silly. Call us anytime day or night," said Thomas.

"Take one day at a time and keep in touch with your family and friends," said Marlene.

"Yes I must get on with my hobbies," said Rosemary as brightly as possible.

Two months later Rosemary was watching the bobbing of daffodils from her dining room window. The forsythia was in full golden bloom. Things were getting back to normal she mused. She was back at Scrabble Club, doing a little gardening, visiting Glenda.

However without self-scrutiny she eased two place mats on to the table, as ever, added shining clean cutlery, two glasses and napkins on to the freshly laundered red tablecloth, because some things would not change for a long time.

REMOVING THE STING

It's strange that I cannot see down the corridor from my bed, but I imagine it clearly. I hear the cries of a drunken patient echoing along it as he is confronted by a member of staff showing great forbearance and discipline. Then there is a whiff of disinfectant intermingled with the more pungent smell of stale urine. I imagine there being many frequently opened doors leading off the corridor and it being lined by trolleys containing the latest medical technology. There is occasional brusque conversation and shuffling of feet and paper on clipboards.

One sound impinges on my memory more than any other and that is the rhythmic tapping of earnest Nurse Welch's footsteps approaching the ward. I know she will make a proud entry and say "Time for your meds ladies". Step aside! Woe be it if you happen to confront Nurse Welch in the corridor when it's medicine time. I imagine the cleaner with the crooked neck turning his gaze away from the mop and bucket, glancing warily at her flushed visage. Who is next to be admonished for a misplaced trolley?

Nurse Welch was an orphan of the Blitz. She was brought up by a strict aunt, who instilled in her a strong sense of duty and discipline within a traditional feminine role. Her base desires were rather repressed and this led her to be a little domineering to patients and staff. However, nursing to her was a vocation not a job.

Nurse Welch opened the drugs trolley with a haughty officious air and began to distribute our medicine. She was efficient, I grant, but I could not pretend to like her. When she handed me the usual small plastic cup containing my pills, I commented to her that there were three tablets and not the usual two.

She answered rather abruptly, "That's the correct dose," in a manner that made me feel quite estranged, but dutifully I swallowed them.

*

There was a hub-bub on the ward that evening. Mrs Hopkins' son was visiting. He was a rather overbearing and ebullient character and talked loudly to his mother, who was very weak and ill. His wife presented as rather meek and a little subservient. They had brought in a large bundle of yellow roses, which brought a vague smile to Mrs Hopkins' ashen and weary face. She became more alert and less apathetic. I was quietly pleased.

Gradually, visiting time passed and people left the ward in dribs and drabs. I had not expected a visitor tonight and in any I case I began to feel giddy and disoriented as darkness fell and the lights shone brighter. I closed my eyes and tried to relax, it would be a long night. Suddenly, my stomach convulsed, I felt nauseous and breathless and cried out for a nurse to attend. Nobody came immediately, they must all have been busy. "Nurse!" Too late. I vomited violently over the bedclothes and felt relieved for a second and then disgusted with myself for having made such a mess. Events after that I recall only sketchily. I remember a lady in a white coat amidst the rotation of the ward ceiling before my eyes. There were other fuzzy figures bearing down on me. Then everything went blank.

Nurse Julia Welch had little fear of authority but waiting outside the Nursing Officer's room she would admit to apprehension. The Nursing Officer opened the door wearing a stern expression and ushered in Nurse Welch. Julia entered with trepidation having not been invited to the office for six years. The Nursing Officer came straight to the point.

"We have reason to believe that Mrs Evans' sudden relapse was the result of your dispensing her too large a dose of Hyperidine at 1800 hours last evening. Do you have anything to say on the matter?"

For once in her life Nurse Welch was aghast and lost for words. Her vocation. Her chin rested on her neck and a lump stuck in her throat. She felt lost to say anything in her defence. The truth hurt.

"We have no option but to suspend you from your nursing duties until we decide whether you are permitted to return."

*

A light drizzle was falling to make the pavements slippery after a long drought. Nurse Welch stepped outside into the busy street, pulled her cape around her and trudged homeward. She exuded a lugubrious air and such was her despondency, that she was oblivious of the bustle around her. Suspended. A salty taste tinged her tongue as tears dribbled down her blank face.

Suddenly, she was forced to make an abrupt halt as a boy on a bicycle crossed her path at great speed, from a side alley. The youth swerved to avoid her but crashed into a pillar box. Miraculously, Julia was sprung into action at the behest of a burst of adrenaline as the boy crumpled into a heap among the mangled remains of his bicycle.

Quickly, she called for help, managed to lift the boy with a man's assistance and lay the boy down in the recovery position on her cape. The drizzle intensified to steady rain. Blood was pouring from a head wound and she feared and ascertained that the boy was slipping into unconsciousness. By now, there was a posse of bystanders offering advice but Nurse Welch remained calm and authoritative. An ambulance was called while Julia tried to clean the wound with tissues and sterile wipes she always carried in her handbag. She felt for his thready pulse and was forced to begin cardiac massage and mouth to mouth resuscitation. Just as the ambulance arrived, the boy began to breathe shallowly. The paramedics cleared the crowd and did their work.

Nurse Julia Welch gathered herself, rung out her soaking, blood-stained cape and walked onward with a more assured gait towards her flat. She turned the key, collapsed into the chair and eyed a pile of dishes from breakfast time to be cleaned.

When I came round and opened my eyes nervously, bright sunlight slanted through the window illuminating the whole ward in glorious attire. I turned my head and perceived fresh flowers with a delicate scent. Mrs Hopkins was chewing meditatively on a paltry lunch. I felt glad for her and glad to be alive. Her lunch made me feel hungry but I was only too aware of a needle in my arm connected to a drip feed. I had no idea what day it was but the clock read half-past twelve. I recognised Nurse Jones walking softly towards my bed. She took my hand gently and asked how I felt. After five minutes or so she said. "We have news for you Mrs Evans. Unfortunately your son was injured badly in a cycling accident but he is recovering in hospital. Apparently he has a vague recollection of a kind nurse helping him. He promises to visit you in a few days when he is better."

ROSA

Rotund Rosa asks the time. Three minutes to nine.

"When's the bus due?"

"Nine thirteen."

A huge bag stands next to her on the newly laid tarmac. Is she studying at college like me? Yes, piping thick oozing icing from a soft bag on to immaculate cakes, I muse.

Has she cut ruby marzipan hearts? Not yet.

Her coffee-coloured face and tight curls augment her friendly demeanour. The yellow lamplight catches the hint of a smile. Her sensible shoes and plain tights suggest diffidence. To me she exudes stoicism. I can think lazily that she has a husband and six children in her care.

A sneaky breeze soughs the stunted whips around the bus stop. There is a long silence.

"I'm at college too, creative writing."

"You going to write a book?"

That flattens any cockiness.

"I doubt it, but Bob here and I are having fun. We have enough money to manage."

She offers a resigned look which suggests money is tight. We speak no more. She's grounded me in her world, yet she has the kind of patience which I hope secretly she has seen in me. She eyes me warily, coughs drily and squashes any lingering intrigue I may have invented. She is the embodiment of ordinary, coping womanhood in a world outside of my egocentric whims which I'm allowed via state benefits.

"You see to Paul for a while, I'll do the observations and look out for them."

"O.K."

Jim opens a can of soup, his anxiety leading him to spray his pullover with small orange blobs. More carefully he empties the contents into a small pan, lights the gas stove and stirs. His ears are hurting and his brain feels too big for his skull. The torment of Paul's groaning and the thunderous crashing of water straps him in claustrophobically to this perilous existence.

Jack climbs the metal stairs ponderously, mindful of Paul's fate, 32, 33, 34, out on to the gantry he steps trembling now. The wind howls in a ghostly tone and the grey ocean is frenzied and unforgiving. Jack gauges that visibility is no more than fifty metres as curtains of drizzle pepper the large window. Jack decides to switch on the light to guide the rescuers and console his brotherly nature towards Paul. He takes a notebook from his pocket and promptly drops it on to the cold and slippery gantry. Having retrieved it he scribbles *7C, WbyN 11, 995mb, Rising Quickly, 50m*, peering at the electronic display below the light. Surely they will be here soon. Jack scours the sky for that merciful black dot that would be an approaching helicopter.

Jim pours out the soup into a large metal mug. He steps softly towards the bedroom door as Paul's groaning and muttering gets ever louder. The door creaks open and the abiding incongruity of a rectangular bed in a circular room flashes momentarily across Jim's mind.

"Some soup mate. They should be here soon."

Paul's face is ashen, small beads of sweat smatter his brow. His glazed eyes squint. A makeshift sling hangs from the ceiling holding his blooded right leg.

"It's bloody agony, mate," he shouts above the roaring of

waves. The room is dusky, the tiny window washed intermittently by raging sea water.

"I'll bring some aspirin and some water," says Jim scratching his beard nervously as he contemplates the job that the rescue crew have ahead of them.

Jack feels a wave of relief rush through him. The helicopter hovers like a wasp above a juicy plum below the enveloping cloudbase. Purposefully he descends the staircase as fast as safety allows. He bursts through the bedroom door.

"They're in sight Paul, we'll have you out of here soon."

SHEILA

The milky light of the full moon bathed the neatly mown patch of grey sward, damp with dew and surrounded by roses and privet. Here I fell into your arms like an exhausted athlete fighting for air at the end of the race. I entered your private space and you accepted me with loving gifts no dowry could buy. You rose and stumbled and I kept you from falling. How I wish you could have saved me from the muddy morass of the tortured mind, the quicksand on the shores of parting, with the savage silence of love gone cold.

You loved me but no more dear wife. We shall never be able to truly say sorry.

Your memory lingers, sometimes like a lead pendant cutting into my neck and sometimes the enlightening sunrise of experience.

TEPID?

The water drips from the hot tap. The washer has worn through endless hours of turning on and turning off. So much water leaks that each drop is tepid. The beer had been ice-cold when he'd ripped open the refrigerator and grabbed the can from the door. Now it is attached to the work-top by a sticky brown stain, half-full now, tepid, in the suffocating heat of the afternoon.

It's Christmas Eve. Yvette has forgotten to switch the fan off in her worry and hurry to get things done. It whirrs incessantly, wafting the odour of crushed garlic from the chopping board into every nook and cranny of the kitchen.

Yvette will be back from Bourke soon, with trimmings for the festivities; more tepid canned beers, juice, melting ice cream, soft butter, squashy oranges, figs and dates.

She squints through the glare of steely sunlight bouncing in all directions from eucalyptus leaves. The grass is browning and the sheep are emaciated, spiniflex dots the landscape. Yvette fumbles in a packet of aspirin and for her bottle of water and drives with one perspiring hand on the wheel. The car does a zig-zag then she regains control. Emma and Zac are expected at 4pm. Yvette glances at her watch, 3.10pm. Max is having a siesta upstairs at home. Usually he rouses at five to water the sheep.

Yvette speeds up, beads of sweat trickle down on to her sunglasses. The external thermometer reads 41 degrees.

Why does she have to go through this? She wishes Christmas could be postponed.

Yvette parks up in the yard. Emma and Zac are already there.

"Hi Mum, can I help you with that?" says Zac.

"That would be lovely. Hello you two. Let's get inside and cool down."

"Good idea."

"How was the journey?"

"The overnight bit through the mountains was good, but it has been too hot today."

Zac removes his baseball cap. His dark hair is moist and lank and a brown line encircles his crown. He, Emma and Yvette collapse on to the wooden chairs in the kitchen having unpacked the shopping.

"Your father's upstairs. He sleeps from noon till five in summer."

"Why don't you tell him we're here?" said Zac.

"I don't like to disturb him."

"Tell you what we'll pour ourselves a tinny while you rouse him." Zac smiles.

"Oh great deal I must say. I don't really want all this alcohol in the house at the moment."

"Why not Mum? It's Christmas."

"Yes and I've a blinding headache. O.K. I'll rouse him as it's for you."

Reluctantly, Yvette rights herself. Her swollen calves and ankles protesting at every step on the stairs. Out of earshot Emma asks Zac, "Why is your Mum wearing her sunglasses indoors?"

"Search me. She seems to have lost her sense of humour too."

Yvette returns thudding down the stairs with greater urgency than she ascended.

"Strange," she says in as credible a tone as possible. "There's some drawers open and he's not there. I didn't see the Land Rover when we came in. Zac could you check it's not around?"

"Sure will. Have you got something wrong with your eyes Mum? You're still wearing your sunglasses."

"My eyes are tired and there's a lot of pollen."

While Zac and Emma go to search for Yvette's husband in the outbuildings, Yvette nips into the bathroom. Before the mirror she lifts her sunglasses to reveal an angry purple bruise around her left eye. Trembling she reaches for cosmetics.

THE BEAUTIFUL BRINY, SHIMMERY SHINY

Jeff began to ascend the hill and around the bend he spied the brown sign *Giants Causeway 11miles.* His mobile phone rang. There was nowhere to pull over. A patchwork of meadows extended down to the cliff and the summer sunshine glinted brightly on the waves as the strange incongruous outline of Rathlin Island jutted up from the deep. As Jeff reached the crest of the hill, he could see the huddle of white painted houses that was Portrush in the far distance.

Jeff was taking a holiday alone, which might have seemed an unusual decision given that he was deeply depressed, but interaction was difficult for him these days.

Fortunately, his profession as an accountant magnified his strengths in dealing with figures, paperwork and officialdom. But in recent months he had spent less time in conversation with clients and more time in his cosy, comfortable office. That was until his boss told him to take some leave and sort himself out.

Jeff preferred to wear sunglasses; they hid some of his despair. He was wearing them today, which given that it was a glorious day, would not appear the slightest bit unusual to others. Jeff wore his sunglasses on cloudy days, admittedly not for driving but in all other daytime pursuits and when out of an evening. If anyone questioned him about it he would lie that he was partially sighted. The only other place in which Jeff didn't wear his sunglasses lately was back in the office.

Jeff's mobile rang again just as he turned down the narrow lane that descended to the car park above the Giants Causeway. Again he was unable to answer it. Jeff had hired his car from a dealer in Belfast, where he had left his vehicle for the week.

"Hello, ah Mum." Jeff had parked up near the gift shop at the geological attraction on the north coast of Northern Ireland.

"Not too bad."

"I could come over Thursday week."

"Good to hear it, I'll probably go with Eurostar. I'll give you the times etcetera when I get back."

Jeff's mother lived in Paris with her second husband Pierre, a rotund, moustached, stereotypical Frenchman with oodles of charm and wit. Jeff had not taken to him immediately finding him a little superficial for his own spiritual demeanour, but their relationship had improved during the dozen times Jeff had travelled to Paris.

There was nothing, however, to replace Jeff's father, the source of all youthful encouragement and solace through a difficult teenage life and Jeff's moral foundation. Jeff's father had died of emphysema six years ago and Jeff had admitted to his therapist that he had never really recovered from the loss. In truth, Jeff had buried a lot of his emotional trauma into his work. He had great difficulty in accepting, at first, that his mother had another man especially when Laura had relocated to France three years ago.

A brisk sea breeze struck up and whipped up vortices of dust around the car park. Jeff stayed in his seat absorbing the scene contemplatively. Jeff had the idiosyncrasy of taking his toothbrush on excursions, together with a mug, paste and small flannel. He was not averse to using them in public toilets and this occasion was no exception. Languidly, he left his car as if parting with an old friend but paced purposefully to the Gents. Jeff did think that perhaps bringing his own water bottle might be more hygienic but he liked the feeling that everything was washed away by the tap.

Jeff patted his face dry and headed back briskly to his car. The sun had passed behind cumulus cloud and it felt distinctly cooler.

Jeff decided to walk down to the Causeway and proceed further to the Organ Pipes rather than taking the shuttle bus, as he had made a ninety minute journey from the guest house in Belfast and needed to stretch his legs.

Harriet Loftus was staying with her friend Janet, whom she had met in Coleraine whilst studying midwifery. She, Harriet, was now studying obstetrics, partly at the University of Coleraine and partly at the local maternity unit. Janet was a Registered General Nurse at Coleraine Hospital. They had decided to take a short holiday together, as with some persuasion of the NHS Trust, they had managed to obtain leave together for four days.

Harriet had not travelled widely in Ulster and desired to see the Glens of Antrim, the Mourne Mountains and the Giants Causeway. The Causeway was less than an hour's drive from Coleraine but Janet and Harriet had such busy lives that they had never fitted a visit into their itinerary, until this crisp, bright afternoon in June, which was rare in this part of the world. They chatted away happily in Harriet's car, which was modest in size because Harriet was having to pay tuition fees at University. She could only keep it on the road with financial assistance from her parents who lived in the unpretentious town of Newtonards in Down. Harriet and Janet would visit Harriet's parents on the way to the Mourne Mountains tomorrow and see the Glens of Antrim on their third day together.

After a long pause Janet broached a subject that was troubling her. "Why doesn't a vivacious, skilled woman like yourself have a boyfriend?"

"Perhaps I've not met the right person, who would allow me to continue my career without any distraction or manipulative behaviour. I prefer your company than any man's."

"You're not becoming a lesbian are you?"

"No I'm not. Don't put two and two together so narrow-mindedly Janet. I just enjoy doing things for our sisterhood. If that sounds a bit high-falooting then let it be."

Janet looked straight ahead feeling she'd overstepped the mark. She folded her arms across her chest. To defuse the situation she asked no more personal questions that afternoon. Inside, she felt disconcerted and irritated as a conversation like this had reared up only a week before and she was no nearer getting a decent answer from her friend on what seemed like a straightforward issue. Harriet rarely spoke to a man outside work and there was just one male obstretician at work.

As they passed through Portrush, a cooling breeze struck up. Janet and Harriet closed their side windows. Climbing up out of the town, the sea beyond had become choppy with white horses and spray like fumaroles issued up the cliff. Eventually they parked with some difficulty at the Giants Causeway because there were many visitors on that fresh cool afternoon.

Janet inspected her make-up in the mirror of her compact. Harriet wore little make-up but brushed her hair looking in the rear-view mirror.

"Surely you'll need to brush it when you get back out of this wind," nagged Janet.

"You're getting on at me again. I thought we were going to have a good afternoon out. I hope this is not going to last all four days."

Janet sighed loudly and crossed her arms across her chest again. Harriet noticed her crestfallen friend and said, "Come on let's get an ice cream and walk down. We can look in the gift shop afterwards, I could buy you something for your birthday."

"That would be nice," replied Janet.

Both women hopped out of the car briskly, locked up and went to queue for their ice creams. Jeff Durston was on his return from the cliff walk to the Organ Pipes and was nearing the Causeway itself. A curtain of approaching virga hung below slate grey cloud over the sea despite there being only three oktas of cloud in the sky.

Janet and Harriet licked their ice creams as they descended the road to the Causeway, at one point having to continue single file as a shuttle bus rumbled past them carrying less mobile visitors. The hexagonal blocks of basalt were worn into moulded, shallow dishes by the feet of hundreds of thousands of previous visitors and occasional incursions from stormy seas.

Janet had brought her camera, slung around her neck, and Harriet posed for a few photographs while the thoughtful Jeff Durston stepped gingerly up and down with the geometry of the pillars. Harriet wanted a final shot to be taken at the seaward end of the Causeway, near the water's edge. Here the basalt pillars were moist and slippery. Jeff Durston was close now and he eyed Harriet through his sunglasses as the breeze from the sea strengthened. Just as Janet clicked her camera, after manoeuvring into the best possible position, a much larger wave crashed over the seaward end of the Causeway. Harriet lost her footing and with an anguished cry was swept into the tumult.

Jeff turned quickly and scampered down to the water's edge as Harriet's head bobbed in and out of the water. In an instant he stripped off his jacket and shirt and hurried into the waves. Jeff swam out towards Harriet more strongly than he could have imagined possible, at the behest of the adrenaline surging through his body. He reached Harriet and muscled her head above the water while he swam backstroke with one arm back to the shore, as Janet looked on from the Causeway flabbergasted.

As Jeff and Harriet stumbled on to the rocky shore Harriet vomited violently expelling swallowed sea water, but was breathing and conscious. Jeff collapsed on to some dry pillars having guided Harriet to safety. When Harriet's breathing had returned to normal she croaked "Thank you. You may have saved my life," looking directly into his eyes. Jeff went to retrieve his jacket, shirt and sunglasses. Janet wrapped a comforting arm around her stricken friend. Another large wave surged over the Causeway and nearly engulfed Jeff on his hurried return to the women. Harriet shivered in her sodden blouse and trousers. "I have another T-shirt in my bag in the car," said Janet as Jeff finally reached them. Jeff found it hard to not notice Harriet's deep brown eyes and feminine curves but thought wisely that this was not the moment to pursue the matter.

"Do you mind if I accompany you two ladies to your car, you seem very shaken?"

"We wouldn't mind at all. You must be very cold too," said Janet.

Harriet stood up gradually unwinding her tired spine and

began to sob quietly. Janet and Jeff comforted her as they picked their way across the landward Causeway and trudged up the roadway to the car park. Thankfully, warm sunshine returned after the squall. Harriet found something extraordinary dawning on her mind as they reached the car park. It was that possibly there were respectable men in the world. For his part, Jeff felt that the incident had jolted his depression and had galvanized him into believing that he was capable of action above the melancholic musing which had held sway over his mind for some weeks.

Harriet was extremely surprised and Janet almost as astounded when Harriet handed Jeff her phone number as they parted for their respective homeward journeys.

Harriet squeezed out her trousers in the Ladies toilet with Janet at her side.

"Well, that was an adventure we'll never forget," said Janet.

"I'm not sure that was such a good idea giving him my phone number," offered Harriet reflectively.

"I don't know, something positive might come of it," said Janet brightly.

Jeff Durston would have liked to have browsed around the gift-shop for a souvenir of the extraordinary afternoon but he decided to get home as soon as possible to change into some dry clothes. He set off determinedly and drove in a more elated mood than for many months. He thought for the first time, as he descended into Ballycastle, of returning to his office confidently, with his little golden locket of achievement kept secret. He would leave a couple of days for Harriet to recover and phone her on Tuesday. He wouldn't tell his mother anything unless anything more emotionally sustaining came of the whole incident. In fact he wouldn't tell anyone until he had spoken to Harriet again. It wasn't just the subliminal sexual element which made him desire to keep things secret; he didn't want to be seen by family and colleagues as blowing up his whole ego with tales of heroism. Jeff was a thoughtful man who didn't really like to be the centre of attention, perhaps that made him prey for depression to strike.

His work habits illustrated his diffidence and he was beginning to feel that some new social contacts would be very beneficial as a new wave of positivity washed over him.

Harriet and Janet's friendship was losing some of its previous uneasiness when they returned to Coleraine. Janet, inclined to be critical of Harriet as the archetypal woman's woman, had come face to face with the fact that she could have lost her friend if she spent a minute longer in the water. Janet knew she would have been helpless to act being so far from the waterline. The mystery of Jeff had hung between them on the journey home. He really did present as thoughtful and unassuming in the little time they had spent together.

Having Janet around had allowed Harriet the comfort of not having to tell everyone she had been rescued. She might otherwise have bottled it up and then blurted in one egocentric explosion when on the defensive. Harriet had become marginally more empathetic towards the male obstretician at college and she had spoken to her wayward brother on the telephone for the first time in three months. To preserve the lives of mothers and babies had become an even greater pre-occupation having swung on the thread of her own vivacity and Harriet thrived in her work.

"Hello. Is that Harriet?"

"Speaking. Is that Jeff?"

"Have you recovered a bit?"

"Yes, thank you. I'm back at work on Thursday. I love my work."

"Wish I was so happy in mine, but I should be back soon. I'm feeling a bit better now."

Jeff had told Harriet and Janet that he was signed off work with ill health on the way back to the car park at the Giants Causeway. Initially he had regretted it because it drew unwanted attention to a problem, but Harriet and Janet took him as they found him and he was pleased.

"I wondered whether you had anything planned for this weekend?"

"I'll probably see Janet and some pals on Sunday and I visit my parents Sunday evening but Saturday evening is free."

"If it's not impertinent, would you like to come out to a restaurant of YOUR choice as I don't know Coleraine that well."

"I would like that. I can direct you."

Jeff and Harriet spent most Saturday evenings together for the next three months and got to know each other better. Jeff became a little frustrated that Harriet did not want to show him much affection, but he remained patient as she was smart, reliable and interesting. Initially, Harriet was perturbed by Jeff's insistence on wearing sunglasses and his brushing his teeth at every venue they attended, but he grew out of it as he gained in confidence and returned to work. Harriet felt mature enough not to divulge every little detail of their relationship to Janet and her friends, who were eager to hear everything. She did tell her mother during their long conversations on Sunday evening. Harriet's brother Colin visited her for the first time in five years and they talked like grown-ups again.

One fine weekend in October Jeff and Harriet went to Paris. They booked into an affordable hotel and arranged to meet Jeff's mother and stepfather at a café near Notre Dame. Jeff was apprehensive about the impression his jocular but unpredictable stepfather would leave on Harriet.

"Would you like Laura and I to show you around the Louvre, the Tuilleries and visit the Eiffel Tower tomorrow?" said Pierre enthusiastically.

"Perhaps Harriet and Jeff would like to explore by themselves and have time for themselves," interjected Laura.

Laura had always exhibited sensitivity and tact and Jeff loved her for it despite her obsessive cleanliness at home.

"Well let me get you a bottle of the very best French to thank you for coming," continued Pierre, undaunted by his wife's reticence.

"Just one glass would be lovely, Pierre," said Jeff. "Harriet doesn't drink very often."

Harriet nodded and said "Just one please."

Pierre chatted fervently about the rights and wrongs of French society and how he and Laura had had to tighten their belts during the economic recession, while they enjoyed a glass of wine. "A toast to you both," he finished and they clinked glasses.

Soon it was time for Jeff and Harriet to wend their way to the hotel. "Bon Voyage, Entente Cordial, Love and Peace," exclaimed Pierre as he rose to his feet. Laura pecked both of them on the cheek. Pierre gave them suffocating bear hugs and beamed warmly below his luxuriant moustache. Jeff felt more relaxed now that the meeting had passed off well. Harriet felt relaxed too and took Jeff's hand for only the third time since they had met. They wandered inquisitively among the pavement artists on the banks of the River Seine.

When they reached their hotel room Harriet kissed Jeff's succulent lips quite spontaneously then pulled back and gasped, confused and stunned by the moment.

Jeff responded by hugging her gently and kissing her cheeks, nose and lips. During foreplay Jeff treated Harriet like a prize piece of porcelain and to her surprise Harriet relaxed completely and enjoyed their tender lovemaking. As they lay together in the enveloping warmth of their duvet, as a Parisian dusk fell, Harriet faced Jeff and lifted his chin with her fingertips.

"Jeff there is something I want to tell you."

"I'm all ears dear."

"You may have noticed that I always fling myself into my midwifery with great enthusiasm and have been cagey about you touching me over the past three months."

"Well, I noticed a little, but honestly it didn't bother me."

"One of the reasons is that, six years ago I was raped outside the hospital in Coleraine and I had an illegal abortion."

Jeff kissed her ever so softly on her lips and realised that he was an extremely privileged man.

THE BRIGHT LIGHT OF HOPE

Ryan strode forward from midfield. He could smell his marker's breath, hear the rattle of phlegm in his throat. Sweat streaked Ryan's neck. He heard David's call from the wing, the murmur of the ball bobbling across the slippery Astroturf. He swung a foot.

It pinged off his boot satisfyingly. The crowd clapped and cheered. Was that Mum and Dad he heard among them? Ryan felt an arm wrap around his neck, he knew it was Michael, likewise Matthew's familiar patting on his back. Surely there were just seconds to play. England were going to win.

I remember the backyard at 14, Cross Street, Dagenham. The feel of little bits of gravel under my pumps and the vague whiff of cat's pee in the far corner. That warm Saturday morning, my brother Kevin was bouncing the ball making a pleasant rhythmic but impatient thudding, while mother held me in her arms and her lips made a little warm damp mark on my cheeks.

"Kevin's taking you to Redbridge Common to play with the older boys on grass, as his birthday treat."

"Great."

"Hurry up Ryan." The thudding had stopped. I stepped out, feeling the warmth of the sun on my neck.

Dad was more distant than Mum. From what he said over the years, I gathered that he was a tad embarrassed by me. That morning though he had been cheerful for a change. He had poured the milk over my porridge and had put a handful of raisins, I think they were, on the top. I delighted in the tastes of my food and Mum said I ate grown-up things like mushrooms and garlic when other children had lots of sweets.

Mum and Dad had bought me new football kit. I could feel the silkiness of the brand new polyester, Mum called it, on my chest and thighs, and the snugness of my new cap. Anyway, Kevin took my arm and we walked out into the fume-laden air. Kevin said he couldn't smell much, but I could. From a distance I heard Peter calling me.

"Hiya Ryan, coming to play?" I heard the crunching of grit under his running feet.

"You're magic Ryan. Fancy banging in some of my crosses?"

"As long as they're not too hard. I don't want to be knocked over. You're all bigger than me."

"Na, you won't be. Don't be a wuss. Here fancy a Wrigley? Nice new kit."

"Thanks Pete."

I asked Kevin the time.

"Can we play for an hour?"

"Maybe Ryan, I've got some work to do on my bike this afternoon."

Soon I could feel the crunching and crackling of dry grass on the common. It hadn't rained in ages. It was a great hour there, being a respected contemporary of ordinary men. My long journey had begun. I remember that day as it were yesterday. How Mum had made me a birthday cake when we got home. The acrid smell of the candles I was guided to blow out. Licking the cake mix off the spoon. Over the years I'd made a mental map of the kitchen and Mum was quite happy for me to find the knife and cut the soft spongy cake. In the afternoon I was entertained by the clinking and rattling of Kevin dismantling his bike and the sound of my new Simple Minds CD *Real Life.* Best of all was my Dad, who worked long shifts at Ford and was often tired, giving me a big bear hug before tea. After that my confidence seemed to lift for ever.

THE EVENING WATCH

It is 5.45pm and the cabinets are being locked. I reach the corner cabinet and peruse the exhibits carefully. I think it takes a certain meticulous streak to work in a jewellers. I notice that a gentleman's dress watch is missing from the middle shelf of the cabinet.

"Jane, have we sold a gents' dress watch today?"

"Not that I know of. I'll go through the computer record on the till if you could finish locking up, Julie."

I love looking at the glinting sparkling stones under the trendy spotlamps. I stop to feel them when opening up and closing. My boss Jane tells me to hurry up but I am transfixed. My suspicions are aroused now and I check over each cabinet with the utmost care. As far as I can tell nothing else is awry; the cabinets at our jewellers are restocked every day so why should we be an exhibit short?

Generally our stock is out of my price range but perhaps James will buy me a small treat for Christmas. He says I should think more of the suffering of gold, silver and platinum miners in poor countries and less of the fat wallets of the dealers in Rotterdam. He likes to buy me something more practical for my birthday like a warm coat or boots.

Last night at the supper table we were sitting in silence for a couple of minutes enjoying lasagne and steaming hot broccoli when …

"Good day again Julie, the water pump project in Niger seems to be bedding in. We've teamed up with VSO and eight new water pumps were installed last week, apparently the taps are running great. A lot of houses in Pakistan have been repaired after the floods and new villages are springing up, same thing in Sri Lanka after the recent floods. We've been there in force since the tsunami. I know it seems a long time ago but we've stuck it out through thick and thin putting roofs over people's heads. Pity Australia might have to sort themselves out..." And so it goes on.

Don't get me wrong I love James dearly, he is a man of great compassion and enthusiasm, but we never talk about my work. I resent him hogging the moral high-ground and have even thought of changing my job to appease him. But not for long, I love my job. There is great camaraderie between Jane and us women, I feel a bit sorry for Marcus, being the only man he seems so serious while we laugh and joke. When we are busy time flies.

There is a nagging doubt in my mind that I might lose James. He's so handsome and cheerful and good in the sack, maybe if I buy him a nice dress watch he would appreciate the craftsmanship and loving gesture. Ah, I know your suspicions are aroused reader that it was I who stole the watch but it wasn't me I can assure you.

Jilly, Jade and Pat are the prime suspects in my mind. They all work till 3. I can't imagine a customer having the sleight of hand to take a watch while we attend the cabinets.

"Julie we haven't sold a watch of that sort. I'll have to call the staff to an emergency meeting tomorrow."

So on that Tuesday morning Jilly, Jade, Pat, Sue, Marcus and Julie sat nervously awaiting Jane's diatribe about security. Surprisingly she was quite measured.

"It would be helpful if the culprit owned up now. I'm not going to call the police just now but Head Office have stated that a new security guard called Graham will begin work here tomorrow. If it happens again we shall bring the police in, understood? Has anyone the stomach to own up?"

Jilly screwed up her face, Jade twiddled her fingers, Pat looked down into her lap disconsolately. Marcus stared straight ahead not wanting to catch Jane's eye. I wondered absentmindedly that a security guard would ruin the bonhomie in the shop, as if the theft hadn't done so already.

"Very well, perhaps someone would like to confess to me in private later. We had better open up now it's already 8.50."

At 5.55pm Jane is alone in the shop. She tidies the counter having made herself a strong tea. Her nerve is breaking. This could end up a right mess, after all she has complete control over the finances here. As the bells of Highfield Church chime six she locks the front door of the jewellers and scampers over to the nearest cashpoint in Tower Street. For some reason Jane feels conspicuous as if just everyone is watching her. She taps her PIN glancing over her left then right shoulder. With trembling hands she stuffs five twenty pound notes into her purse then repeats the transaction for another hundred pounds. The bitter rows have stopped for a year now. She is not so fearful. This idea of a peace offering seemed a good idea. They are conversing more than ever and even smiling a little.

Jane unlocks the jewellers door again and enters. A man walking briskly with a briefcase seems to be staring at her accusingly. A teenage boy walking the other way spits on the pavement. She rushes up to the counter. She types in the transaction dated for yesterday into the computerised till and slips the £200 into the drawer hurriedly. Is that a sound she hears in the stock room? No it can't be. She'll leave by the backdoor anyway. No-one will be any the wiser.

THE HIGH LIFE

Colin plodded on braced against the unrelenting wind, fine spray stinging his wide moist eyes. The treeless, boggy landscape of the island stretched away to the eastern horizon. Inky clouds trailing menacing virga whipped across from the north west. In the foreground stood an abandoned derelict croft testament to poverty and the Highland Clearances. But Colin was enjoying the freshness of the air arriving from the high Arctic. He'd wanted this holiday for many months, away from the incessant thudding and hissing of machinery at work. The overtime and goggle wearing had made his eyes droop every evening and induced him to nod off before he had prepared his evening meal. Here he would sleep soundly after supper tonight after the invigoration of the fury of the seascape. Colin noticed even the throngs of seabirds were roosting in rocky niches.

Colin quickened his pace as the sun peeked through the ominous clouds. He would have another hour's walk before reaching the guesthouse and Mrs Mackintosh's warm hospitality. A few hailstones bounced off his overcoat and stung his face. Such was Lewis in early April. Colin had met no-one since he left four hours ago and he'd eaten the packed lunch kindly given him at least two hours ago.

An unease flickered across Colin's mind, this was all a bit too forlorn. He missed Maureen. He could have travelled with his friend Ross but when he'd thought it over that may not have been a good choice. Ross had a habit of talking flippantly and telling jokes that only he laughed at. Ross wouldn't appreciate this landscape, probably much preferring to chat to Mrs Mackintosh's daughter Fiona at the guesthouse.

Colin's flat in a tower block in Springburn was pleasant and airy. It was painted in pastel shades of blue and rose. The bespoke tartan carpet was clean, cheerful and augmented by two good quality Afghan rugs in the sitting room. Also in the sitting room was a hand-me-down chestnut bureau in which Colin kept photographs of his ex-wife Maisie, odd snippets from magazines, invoices and bills and a few articles of interest from the *Glasgow Herald* and *The Scotsman.*

The view from the sixteenth floor showed a panorama of Clydeside with cranes jutting up like iron fingers on the river bank, other tower blocks like oversize lego buildings peppered around the city. The ant people scurried around the streets alighting from matchbox buses. Sometimes the tower would seem to sway in storms and Colin could observe rain coming from the far distance. Yet, he often felt cosy playing his acoustic guitar softly enough not to annoy Maureen his nearest neighbour across the hall. She was a fifty year old spinster badly wanting to be rehoused because she had difficulty with lifts and stairs now that she was morbidly obese. This was partly genetic and partly because of a penchant for take-away meals, brought by her sister Janie, and a liking for Coca-Cola.

Colin popped over for an hour or two on a Sunday afternoon to play cards and share memories of his married life in Drumchapel and to listen to Maureen eulogising about her family and her old pet dog Sam whom she missed greatly. They indulged in a wee dram or Irish coffee but neither were hardened drinkers. Colin often wondered when Maureen last had a holiday and cogitated over whether he could ask her to accompany him. In all honesty he would have to nurse Maureen through her holiday. Then he thought how terrible it was that Satan could put such a condescending thought into his head. Nevertheless he had nothing to lose.

"Maureen," he said seriously one sultry Sunday at the beginning of July. Maureen turned her attention from her whist hand to the unreadable look in Colin's blue eyes, then downed the last of her whisky.

"Yes Colin."

"Would you consider coming on holiday with me?"

"That's a kind offer Colin. But what about my legs. I can't walk very far. I'd hold you up while you'd want to go places."

"It could be a coach holiday in the Highlands, you could at least enjoy the scenery and stay on the coach when you make friends to chat to while I'm gone. I might get bored of buying tartan teddies for Donald and Alistair."

Maureen thought hard looking down at her puffy swollen ankles.

"You know Colin I feel so fat and ugly that people won't talk to me."

"You'll have me and maybe you'll have the chance to try some different food."

"I like Coke and burgers, how much would it cost to buy fancy food?"

"You would just have to buy your lunch."

"Colin, I haven't been on holiday for thirty years. Mum and Dad took us to Ayr for a week in 1980 I think it was. I've still got the snaps. I was a size ten then. I remember we played crazy golf near the sea front and there was a wee train to ride on. I dropped my ice-cream when I had an argument with Mum over whether she would let us go skinny dipping in May. The ice-cream man gave me a fresh one, that was kind."

"You've a few good memories haven't you Mo? I'm sure you'd enjoy another break from these four walls."

Maureen surveyed the magazines on her table and the washing-up she'd left since lunch. Her eyes watered and appeared glassy and she fixed Colin's kind eyes again.

"You know I might give it a try. Maybe soon before the council rehouse me."

"You've nothing to lose Mo, I have a week off in August, maybe we could go then. You know I get fed up with the noise at work. I've asked to be transferred to the paint shop. The Union is helping to fix up some more training for me. I'm nearly always up in the Highlands when I've got leave. The flat gets a bit neglected. The cooker needs cleaning and everything's a bit dusty."

Maureen looked after Colin's keys while he was away but she didn't pop in as often as she could as she struggled to keep her flat up together.

"My clothes are getting a wee bit threadbare," said Maureen ruefully. "Perhaps we could go to some charity shops and get some more. The big shops don't have my size and I can't afford these mail-order companies."

"Perhaps Janie could go with you, she'd know more about women's clothes than me."

"I don't like to worry Janie, she's got Callum now and she is already food shopping for me on Mondays."

"Is there anyone else you could ask, work's tough the noo?"

"Please could you come with me Colin, perhaps I could have a go at some dusting for you."

"O.K I might. It would have to be Saturday afternoon; I've a GMB Union meeting in the morning. I don't want to miss it as they are helping me."

Maureen usually lay in late on a Saturday morning but this morning she had set her alarm for nine. After having taken an extra sleeping tablet and some Valerian she had slept a little better than usual. She made herself some porridge, left the pan in the sink to soak, then slipped into Colin's flat using the key he had left her.

Colin's flat was good deal tidier than hers but obligingly she retrieved a dusting cloth from the cupboard underneath the kitchen sink, dampened it and set about cleaning Colin's nick-nacks in the sitting room. A smile flashed across her face as she thought of going away on holiday. She was determined to save a few pounds towards her spending money in the four weeks before they were due to go. She had also put aside £40 from her benefit for some new clothes.

Mo avoided touching four photos of Colin's two children on top of his bureau but was drawn to an envelope marked with an NHS logo on the sitting room table. She was curious enough to have a look inside despite knowing it was wrong to snoop. A fine tremor coursed through her hand as she read its contents.

Dear Mr McKenzie,
You are invited to an appointment at the Hepatic Clinic of Glasgow Royal Infirmary at 9.30am on Tuesday 17th August 2012. If you are unable to attend at this time please telephone the Clinic on 0141 628057 to rearrange your appointment.

Maureen paused; that was a week after they were due to go on holiday. Her smile dropped and her eyes moistened. Was Colin a quiet drinker? There was no evidence as such around the flat. Perhaps Colin was seriously ill, even terminally ill. He had been so kind to her for the eighteen months he had lived opposite. A horrid realisation dawned on Maureen that she was being very selfish with regard to Colin. She began to dust fervently and rushed to look for polish under Colin's sink.

THE INTERVIEW

"Here's a pretty pink one, padded as well, try it on love."

"No."

"There's matching knickers too."

"No way am I trying on that gaudy rubbish."

"Christine, we've bought you a smart outfit between ourselves and we're desperately short of money. Be reasonable and try them on."

"Not on your life."

"Listen, we've run out of money Christine, someone here has to get a job or we'll all have to leave."

"What you forget is that I was bloody well born here, you were not. How can I go parading around like a peacock? At least you have tried it and rejected it, why shouldn't I?"

"Well you haven't got long, your interview at the office is at 10.30 tomorrow, so I suggest you grow up and try on your outfit upstairs."

Christine held her head in her hands and sobbed softly.

"You sleep on it love. I'm sure you'll feel differently in the morning."

"I won't . . . I know I won't . . . but . . . but perhaps I'll try it if it keeps us going."

Mary put her arm around her daughter's shoulder knowing deep down that in Christine's shoes she would feel mortified and afraid at having to go for an interview in the cut-throat world of competition and business. She herself enjoyed the peace and seclusion from it all at the Manor.

Christine accepted a cup of Horlicks from her mother and trudged lugubriously to her room. It would be a long night of tossing and turning, she thought, and so it turned out to be.

The moon shone down through the curtains for a large part of the night, its milky light illuminating the remaining autumn leaves into dusky buff hues. Four times Christine left her bed and peeped out through the curtains. Once a fox darted through the garden its eyes like jewels. Another time a badger loped through the undergrowth. At least at night and at the weekends she could be herself, Christine mused. But why should she take on the responsibility of breadwinning just because she was the youngest of the seven?

At seven o'clock Stefan tapped on the door bringing Christine tea in a china mug. As he set it down on the bedside table, Christine looked into his soft brown eyes and grew nostalgic.

"Do you remember the swinging tree when you were ten and I was five, Stefan? You were a proper big brother to me when you could have been such a bully to your juniors. Stefan you were just perfect."

"Perhaps that happens in nuclear families, I don't know really Christine. But when you're chucked together the more you need to co-operate, 'specially at places like this."

"How do you think like that at this time of morning?" said Christine rubbing her red puffy eyes.

"Probably because my head's turned off by supper time," said Stefan chuckling as he reached for the doorknob.

Christine stared at the clothes draped over the chair that Mary had slipped in late last night. Christine began to feel sympathy for those who had had to wear corsets and crinolines. It must have been like being in prison.

Christine dressed slowly before drawing back the curtains to reveal a foggy first of November. She noticed droplets hanging on and dripping from the red wooded Cornus the name of which always slipped her tongue.

Christine was aware of tautness and discomfort around her waist as she entered the kitchen to join Stefan, John and Mary for breakfast.

"I should enjoy these eggs," said Mary. "They may be the last for a little while. We've two broody and one not laying already."

"Thank you Mary." Christine began to eat her poached egg on toast ponderously while Stefan and John discussed the plastering they needed to do and had their usual moan about Robert not being able to get up in the morning.

Fifty minutes later after the Manor meeting Christine and John emerged from the front entrance of the Manor into swirling mist to make the two kilometre journey to Newlands Ltd regarding the secretarial job for which Christine was to be interviewed. Christine's brow was damp and her hands clammy as she opened the passenger door. John was the only person at the Manor to own a vehicle and because there was urgent plastering to do it was agreed that Christine would catch the bus back. It stopped near the end of the Manor's drive.

Christine had learned some office skills while at the Manor through a correspondence course and the rather old computer they possessed.

"I think it will be a bit hi-tech for me," she said to John as he pulled out of the driveway on to the main road.

"Give your best, Chris," said John soothingly. "There will probably be three interviewers, but try not to be intimidated."

The sun's disc appeared ghostly through the thinning mist as John dropped Christine off at Newlands Ltd, illuminating the façade of the building in the palest of yellows.

"Good luck Christine. All the best."

"Thank you I'll need it."

Christine tottered up the steps to the reception in the slightly ill-fitting medium high heels that Mary had given her. The reception was surprisingly modest but the receptionist was turned out immaculately with perfect white nails, clean shiny black hair and big brown eyes. She was tall and slim with pink glossed lips.

"Good morning . . . I am here to be interviewed for the post of secretary to Mr Thomas," managed Christine as a bead of perspiration crept down her forehead.

"Ah yes madam, I shall let him know you are here. Your name is?"

"Christine McEvoy."

Five minutes later a well-groomed Mr Thomas appeared from a side corridor. He smiled broadly and extended his right arm to show the way to the interview room.

"Miss McEvoy please come this way," he said, his smile edging towards a toothy grin.

As they walked Christine smelled a whiff of expensive after-shave and noticed large extravagant cuff links gleaming in the bright overhead light.

Mr Thomas ushered Christine into a large room with deep sashed windows overlooking a well-kept garden. Two women were seated either side of a big padded chair into which Mr Thomas sank with an over exuberant flourish.

"May I introduce Miss Riley and Mrs Cooper," said Mr Thomas, a gold tooth glinting.

Christine sat facing them in a more modest chair, the waist of her skirt digging into her stomach as she tried to take some deep breaths and settle herself. An imposing oak table separated her from her interviewers who smiled rather smugly Christine thought.

"We see you have learned office skills via a correspondence course," said Mr Thomas drily.

"You have never attended college or have any experience in this type of employment."

"That is correct," replied Christine quietly, trying to meet his eyes rather than looking downwards. The gaze from his big brown eyes was quite alluring. Christine began to tap her right foot nervously, hands clasped in her lap, palms moist. She was itching to adjust her bra strap which was about to slip from her narrow shoulders.

Miss Riley and Mrs Cooper plied her with banal questions which Christine answered courteously without rambling, then quite abruptly Mr Thomas brought the interview to a close and the two women vacated the room as Mr Thomas snapped his file shut.

"The interview is now over Miss McEvoy. Thank you for your time, we shall be letting you know soon of the outcome."

Christine got up to leave when Mr Thomas eased around the oak table towards her.

"Can I call you Christine, I'm Stephen," he said smoothly.

Christine looked into his eyes and surveyed his strong jaw and broad shoulders. He was a tall well-built man.

"Yes, I suppose you could," she stuttered.

"Perhaps I could take you to my place to show you more of how the business works before I drop you home."

"I was planning to take the bus actually."

"It will not take long, I live only three minutes' drive away."

"Yes ... well O.K. then," said Christine not exactly sure of what she was up to, but falling for the charm of this confident well-spoken man.

They walked down a flight of stairs and out of sight through the back door to the car park. There was a remnant of mistiness, but the sun was shining brightly as the time approached midday.

Stephen opened the passenger door for Christine and she slid into an extremely comfortable seat in Stephen's Peugeot. As Stephen pulled away Christine said in a quiet voice, "Can you tell me now whether I got the job?"

"I'm afraid I can't Christine, we have another lady to interview this afternoon, but we thought you did rather well," said Stephen letting the steering wheel recoil between his large tanned hands.

Christine noticed no ring on his left hand as he ascended through the gears. As they pulled up outside a detached, white painted house with an imposing blue-painted door, Christine felt slightly dizzy and disoriented, her shoes were hurting her feet. For the first time in her life she felt a strange tingling sensation in her breasts. As they walked towards the door her stomach churned and she felt a tightness across her abdomen.

Stephen unlocked the door and slid his left arm lightly around her back as they entered a surprisingly warm tiled hall. No sooner had the door clicked to than Stephen clasped her to him and began kissing Christine softly on the lips, quickly moving down her neck adorning it with light pecks. Despite enjoying the intimacy, Christine felt confused and apprehensive. Stephen cupped her right breast in his fingers feeling it swell slightly. Christine eased away from him instinctively, there was something not quite right here.

Stephen gazed into Christine's eyes.

"Are you O.K.?"

Christine released eye contact.

"I thought we had business to discuss and I'm afraid I need the toilet."

"It's just down the hall," said Stephen, flatly unable to disguise his frustration. "I'll wait in the lounge there."

Christine could stand no more. She scampered to the toilet and three minutes later crept back around the lounge door, stark naked and shaking visibly. Stephen leaped from his chair his hands trying to caress her curves.

"You've made a bold move, thank you," he whispered in her ear.

"Stephen," she replied grasping both his hands. "There is something I must tell you."

"What's that? You look beautiful."

"I was born … I was born into naturism. I want you to take me home now."

Stephen's arms dropped with his jaw. A grimace flashed across his face and there was a moment's apoplexic silence.

"But … but it's cold out there," he blustered.

"Just fetch me a gown and take me back to the Manor now, that's all."

THE LIFEGUARD

Waves crash, a child's cry.

The bronzed lifeguard turns quickly, his eyes like eagles' piercing through the tumult at the end of the headland. Momentarily he is frozen and then sinews contract at the behest of the adrenaline surging into his blood. In an instant his muscular frame is sprung. He paces like a gazelle across the wet sand, his footprints briefly moulding the strand behind him.

As onlookers gaze helplessly, his heart wants to leap from his chest. Air rushes into every last pocket of his young spongy lungs.

To the dry sand; he ignores any discomfort. Up the steps he bounds, crashing through the dilapidated green door of the coastguard station. He doesn't know how he has the energy to shout "There's a kid out there on the rocks, George, radio the lifeboat."

His legs buckle like rubber as he slumps awkwardly but gratefully into a waiting chair. Ten agonising minutes later the lifeboat crew launch. Time seems to stand still.

Beads of sweat drop from the lifeguard's face into oblivion, perhaps in a few minutes a child will be saved from the ocean of oblivion.

TOP OF THE WORLD

It was misty and cold. Trungpa put on his childlike smile and passed along the weary and bedraggled line clapping his hands, babbling and shouting in his way of encouragement. We stopped to gather breath from the thin mountain air. The yaks stood motionless and morose not wanting to take another voluntary step, the baggage slopping side to side and digging into even their broad backs. We glugged back mouthfuls of lukewarm and unrefreshing water. I heard someone say just one kilometre, just one kilometre indeed. The sun's disc appeared and seemed to bobble through the streaky mist.

Trungpa returned to the head of the convoy. We were stirred into one final gargantuan effort to reach the top. The crunching of boots and hooves on patches of damp scree punctuated the gasping and blowing of humans and animals alike.

Fifteen minutes later the lavishly decorated Buddhist temple glowed above in the eerie low sunlight. Trungpa chatted excitedly and pointed upward to the incongruous opulence set against the unforgiving landscape. Two yaks sneezed loudly. Prayer flags stretched out in all directions from the ramparts of the shrine room stiffened by frost, fluttering pathetically yet defiantly. Trungpa's face glowed as all five of us collapsed into a collective heap at the top of the mountain.

The views were awe inspiring. Snowy peaks, threads of silver water in the valleys, dark fleeting shadows crossed the stark grey rocks on the other side of the valley. Suddenly Trungpa gesticulated for us to gather inside the temple his voice squealing with urgency. At first we were unsure what was happening but Trungpa gabbled "Soldiers come! Soldiers come!"and waved us in. Trungpa had spotted a caterpillar of Chinese soldiers ascending the other side of the mountain.

*

There were seven monks sitting cross-legged in the shrine room. As we entered, they stood up and ushered us courteously into the temple dining room and brought us offerings of yak butter tea, tsampa and Chang. Our noses were red and our fingers white, we accepted gratefully some form of sustenance however strange it tasted.

The senior monk asked us to stay put while he and the others joined Trungpa outside. When they had gone I suggested to the rest that I would keep watch from the window near the entrance to the shrine room. "That's fine, but be careful," said Robert and the others nodded their tacit approval looking apprehensive to a man.

From the narrow window I could see Trungpa in earnest discussion with two other monks. The other five were talking less animatedly and from the wrapping of arms it was obvious that they were very cold.

After twenty minutes, which seemed to hang like an eternity, the head and shoulders of a soldier popped up above the rocks. Suddenly there were six soldiers carrying rucksacks and AK47 rifles confronting Trungpa who had stepped forward bravely. A yak bellowed, echoing down the valley. A bird of prey circled high above the temple as the first soldier raised his gun to Trungpa's chest. I could just hear what was being said above the moaning of the wind.

"We are decently peaceful we mean no harm to your country," said Trungpa.

"You are parasites," said the soldier. "You spend your time sitting around thinking when the toiling workers of the revolutionary party feed your fat bellies."

"We want freedom to practise our religion."

"Like I said, you don't work, you live off blood, sweat and tears."

"Leave us in peace I beg you. We wouldn't kill a worm."

Trungpa felt the butt of the soldier's rifle dig into his forehead.

Trungpa closed his eyes. The bird of prey shrieked again. Images from his life flashed across his mind.

His mother milking the dris outside the tent. Her warm smile and creased tanned skin.

His father reading to his sister from the single Buddhist book they possessed. His first day at the monastery, his clean new robes, the smiles on the faces of his family and friend Norbu. He thought of the mistakes he had made, the embarrassing moments during his adolescence, his regrets that his sister had not received a formal education.

He hoped now that above all he had been a good Buddhist, done things to the best of his ability if now was the time he would pass on to the next life with a favourable rebirth. The wind billowed his crimson robe, a tiny tear welled in the corner of his eye.

Suddenly the pressure on his forehead was relieved, the soldier lowered his gun.

"You are braver than I thought. Just remember mister that the Party and the socialist brotherhood run this land now." Trungpa and the soldier gazed at each other for a couple of seconds. The soldier beckoned the other soldiers to follow him down the path we had ascended.

WALK

The summits of the Langdale Pikes darkened under fleeting shadows and the valley basked in alluring spring sunshine. Hector Milligan packed his rucksack carefully and methodically as Cilla Milligan stood by the car wearing a stern and mutinous expression.

"Hector, the weather forecast isn't great, it could turn at any moment up there."

"Well I only live once," replied Hector vacantly.

"That's an irresponsible attitude."

"We'll be back before sunset. It's shorter than the last one," said Hector determinedly.

"You're so selfish aren't you, making me wait around at the hotel and worry," retorted Cilla.

"There's plenty to do at Ambleside."

"Do you think I'm going to enjoy myself knowing you're rambling around in the piercing cold with a dicky heart. I give up. I really do."

"Suit yourself, but I want to enjoy what remains of my life. I love it here. We have a First-Aider. See you later."

With that Hector turned his head and joined the party of seven hikers assembled at the bridge across the Great Langdale Beck. Cilla jumped into their car, screeched into a three-point turn and drove furiously back towards Ambleside.

Darren, the First-Aider, greeted Hector with concern.

"Sure you're up to it mate?"

"I'm sure I am," said Hector. "I've packed energy bars, emergency food and plenty of water."

The seven of them set off to climb Mickle Pike passing Dungeon Ghyll Force. The sun popped through the gathering cumulus cloud intermittently and the temperature dropped as they ascended. Brendan, Darren and Hector stopped to admire the gushing sparkling waterfall and took some snaps. Soon, the wind began to stretch Naomi's hair horizontally from beneath her sturdy cap. At first, Hector felt hot in his woollen hat but at greater heights he was only too glad of it, as the moaning wind drowned the scraping of boots on stones and pebbles. Hector glanced at his watch. Cilla had made him promise to phone her at 3pm. It was five past two.

The panorama of Lakeland fells and tarns opened up as the seven intrepid walkers approached the summit. They were unaware of a squall bearing down on the North-West side of the mountain in sinister fashion and at great speed. Within two minutes of them arriving at the summit of Mickle Pike, snowflakes were swirling from angry dark clouds. Bent over sideways Hector scrabbled into his pocket for another energy bar. Darren decided not to dally with viewing as the weather closed in.

"Better go down now," he ordered them as the visibility decreased.

While trudging back along a scree-littered broad ridge Hector looked at his watch.

Two-fifty. In doing so Hector slipped on the moist rocks, his right ankle buckled under his weight and his shin smashed against the jagged terrain. The snow began to abate. Hector yelled out in pain to his comrades of which only Darren was behind him. Darren called the others back, his voice echoing around the hillside as the wind dropped but the cold was still numbing. Darren assessed Hector's injuries briskly and was forced to phone for the Air Ambulance. It seemed clear from Hector's agonised cries that he had broken his leg. The others huddled around Hector with their backs to the wind while Naomi held Hector's hand and tried to comfort him. Brendan gave Darren the Ordnance Survey Grid reference above a rustling of wrappers as everyone tapped their emergency supplies. Darren phoned the switchboard for the Air Ambulance.

"They might be here in twenty-five minutes depending on the visibility," said Darren trying hard to be efficient.

"Could you … could you phone my … wife on that number on my … mmm … mobile, Darren," said Hector tremulous with hurt and cold.

A squally wind struck up around the shivering ramblers but the sun reappeared.

"Mrs Milligan, I'm sorry to tell you that your husband has been injured during our walk."

"Bloody fool. Serves him right! I warned him not to go."

"We think he might have a broken leg, it's not directly his heart trouble. The Air Ambulance has been called, they should just have room to land."

"He has a pacemaker fitted you know. Will the electrics on the helicopter interfere with it?"

"I think not but we have to chance it."

"Which hospital is he going to?"

"Kendal, Mrs Milligan. If all goes to plan we should have him there in forty minutes."

"Tell him I'll be there."

The drone of the helicopter became louder as it approached like a red dragonfly chopping through the fresh spring air; sunlight glinting from its side. It hovered overhead and all the walkers lay flat for a moment in the tremendous surge of wind from its blades.

Two figures emerged from the chopper carrying a stretcher and oxygen. Naomi whispered goodbye to Hector and finally let go of his clammy hand. She, Darren, Brendan and the helicopter crew manoeuvred Hector on to the stretcher as he winced in pain. They immobilised and strapped his leg and carried him hurriedly to the waiting aircraft. The helicopter lifted off and the six remaining hikers breathed a collective sigh of relief as they began their descent in sombre mood. Naomi tried to hide her sobbing.

Cilla Milligan parked untidily at Kendal Hospital, slammed the car door shut and bustled to the reception in Casualty. The arteries in her head throbbed and her cheeks were flushed.

"I'm here to see my husband, his name is Hector Milligan," she spluttered. "He has arrived via the Air Ambulance. He has a pacemaker fitted and I am very worried about him."

"Thank you madam. I'll just see whether his admission is recorded on the system. Uhh, yes he is on the orthopaedic ward but they may not let you visit immediately as he was admitted only ten minutes ago and they may need to sort out traction and intravenous fluids."

"But I'm his wife! What, are you going to ask me for I.D. before I can see him?"

"In all fairness Mrs Milligan, we're not stopping you visiting, but you could show a little patience and I'll buzz the orthopaedic ward and they'll tell you when you can go. Please take a seat and we'll bring you a drink."

Cilla plonked herself down on the nearest seat her head churning. She felt like asking Hector for a divorce but in the present circumstances perhaps that would be an excessively cruel thing to do. Her mind turned to Kevin, wise, easygoing, humorous Kevin, whom she had kept secret from Hector for six months. He had big brown eyes, stylish dress and a laissez-faire attitude to all things including their relationship. Cilla could not get him to make a decision on their future and as much as Hector's finnicky obdurance aggravated her, she was on the verge of dumping Kevin. She wanted a clear-cut future not just procrastination and going with the flow. Should she give Hector one last chance? After all, this latest calamity could keep him off the mountains for a while. If only she could control her temper. At that moment the receptionist called Cilla to the desk and directed her to the orthopaedic ward. Cilla scurried along the corridors following the signs and reached Hector's bedside after having asked directions a couple of times.

Hector looked pale and absent as Cilla had expected but to her surprise he managed a loving smile. Yet Cilla couldn't help herself.

"I told you not to go up there, I'll be wanting a divorce."

"That's no way to speak to a poorly man," offered Hector gruffly.

"It's all of your own making."

"Sure it is, but your attitude isn't helping."

One or two heads turned in the ward.

"Can't you spare a little compassion," said Hector wearily. "I was only doing what I love."

"It would help if you showed me a little love," retorted Cilla.

"I still love you."

"Hector, I have something to tell you. This may not be the time and place for it but it must be said. I'm having an affair."

Hector's eyes met Cilla's. To her astonishment his face displayed not the least bit of reproach. Maybe, Cilla thought, he just wasn't up to it and it dawned on her that her attitude allowed little care.

"The truth is, my dear, that I've been having an affair too."

Cilla's jaw dropped. She was dumbstruck. She had deemed her husband so pig-headed that no other woman would have the time of day for him. There was a stunned silence.

"You know," said Hector languidly. "Maybe it's time for us to wipe the slate clean, start again, no secrecy."

"Would you give up the fell walking?"

"Yes I think I would as long as I get some free rein."

Cilla was beginning to see her husband in a new light. Here he was, at least temporarily disabled and emasculated but trying to appease and reason with her. Cilla gently placed her palm across Hector's knuckles and she could sense the relaxation flowing through him.

"You mean no more affairs for us and trying for each other," offered Cilla.

A reciprocated warm smile crossed their faces. Cilla would visit every day during Hector's recovery.

A MERRY CHRISTMAS

Roger was determined not to succumb. This was his offering to society, his recompense. He felt ridiculous in this red and white outfit and long, white, bristly beard. The children of what seemed to him to be comfortable middle-class parents, jostled and shouted. Roger doled out the presents with a cheery smile while trying to put aside doubts about do-gooders in civvy society and hatching a devious plan.

"Alright Roger?" said Don, his supervisor.

"Suppose so."

"We're moving on to Lenchurch this afternoon, there'll be loads more presents."

Roger wanted to go to his new home, open a beer and sit and watch nature programmes. He used to get some stick inside preferring David Attenborough to rugby.

Then Roger's attention was caught by a young boy who appeared to be alone.

"Is there a present for me, Father Christmas?"

Roger felt a prickling compassion for this meek, pale faced little boy. It was a defining moment. He smiled genuinely at the little boy and looked into his eyes with a certain benevolent sorrow. May be Roger could make this forlorn child a tad happier.

The boy grasped the parcel gratefully and said very quietly "Thank you Father Christmas." In Roger's heart there was a chunk of Christmas cheer.

After the lorry was reloaded with presents Roger had a busy afternoon in Lenchurch.

Santa's modern carriage pulled to a halt in the cobbled market square. This was Roger's home town and he felt comfortable with the familiarity. On the other hand he felt glad to be dressed as Santa in case anyone recognised him as the perpetrator of an armed robbery in the town nine years previously. He had had much time to muse at Her Majesty's leisure how foolish it had been to commit a crime in his home town, if he were to be released back to the area, as indeed looked like happening today.

As the light began to fade on a cloudy, raw December afternoon, Roger gave his last present to a blond-haired toddler with his father. Roger asked Don whether it was O.K. to go home and Don assented.

"I'm not taking the Santa gear off just yet."

"Well someone might need it tomorrow for the High Bedham round," said Don.

"People might recognise me."

"Lenchurch is the only place we could find for you, Rog. Take it off and don't be so daft."

But Roger stepped off defiantly for his first independent night, resplendent in his red and white outfit and attracting giggles and finger pointing from passers-by. Don was in hot pursuit but could not keep pace with the more youthful Roger. Roger gained even more odd looks as he broke into a trot and reached the path leading to his flat.

He fumbled under his garb for his newly acquired keys, entered and slammed the door behind him.

On the doormat Roger noticed a flat gift-wrapped parcel. He also noticed Don approaching up the path. Puzzled, Roger hid the parcel as Don banged hard on the door.

"Open up Rog!"

Reluctantly Roger stepped towards the door and took it off the latch. Don tried to appease.

"Listen Rog, you're starting a new life, you can't go around dressed as Father Christmas forever."

"I'm worried. Wouldn't you be? I'd rather live somewhere else."

"We'll be finding you somewhere soon enough."

"How soon?"

"Within weeks."

"That's not soon enough."

"Look Rog, I appreciate what you've done today and that you didn't want to be recognised. Couldn't you get a wig and glasses?"

"Where from? I've got no money."

"Martin will help you get your benefit. Come on let's get the kit off."

Roger took off his outfit mutinously and handed it over. Don thanked him and slipped him a tenner.

"Get yourself some food son."

"It's a bit late now but maybe Martin could take me to the shop in the morning."

"I'm sure he will." Don shook Roger's hand. "Martin will be round at ten tomorrow to see how you're getting on."

Roger said goodbye to Don and turned his attention to the mysterious parcel. His relatives never sent him parcels, they had moved away soon after the trial. Maggie maybe? No, his sister usually just sent a card. Roger unwrapped it with trembling hands. Inside was a pink, perfumed cardboard box. Roger opened it and there revealed was a block of cannabis resin the size of a large chocolate bar. Roger was first astounded then angry. He was making a new life now. Roger hurled the parcel into the empty bin.

Then it dawned quickly that someone must know his whereabouts and he felt a horrified chill down to his bones. A shiver cascaded down his spine. He lit the gas heater and sat down in front of it eating a packet of stale chocolate bourbons he'd found in the kitchen cupboard. There was some cutlery there too.

Roger tried to sleep that night but in the darkness his fears were amplified. Someone knew he was here. He got up several times to drink water. He'd given up dope. Why had someone sent him such a huge quantity?

Martin arrived punctually the next morning and immediately Roger divulged his fears.

"Why has someone sent me a parcel?"

"Can I see it Roger?"

Roger pulled the parcel out of the bin and handed it to Martin.

"I haven't smoked for three years, that was one of the conditions for my parole after Dougie and I got caught smoking skunk in the toilets."

"Maybe it was for the previous tenant, after all it hasn't got your name on it."

"Can you get rid of it for me?"

"I'll take it to the police station. Listen I need you to fill in some forms."

"But I've got no food here, can't we go the shop first? Don gave me a tenner."

"Come on then."

Roger and Martin walked out to Martin's car. As they pulled away Martin said "You'll get your emergency giro, probably tomorrow."

Roger sped round the Co-op and chose some sensible nourishing items. He was determined to make a good start. Within half an hour Roger and Martin were back at the flat which was gradually warming and the condensation was disappearing from the windows. Roger felt a little better now there was milk in the refrigerator and bread in the bread bin. He filled the forms in with some aplomb that surprised Martin. Roger had learned a lot while in jail. Martin kept the cannabis resin out of sight in his jacket pocket. Martin made to leave. "Don will be round tomorrow to make sure your giro's arrived and to act if it hasn't."

"Thanks for everything Martin."

"Pleasure. We'll need to sort out some furniture."

As he walked quickly to his car Martin smirked. Don and he could be about to have a very prosperous New Year with this amount of skunk.

ALL THAT JAZZ

To this it is difficult to dance,
But open your ears if you have the chance.
To the sonorous rhythm of the double bass,
Leads the piano and sax to swiftly chase.
Out of the order to indulgent tinkling,
And the drum with guitar strings sprinkling,
Fuel on the fire of musical tangents,
There is basic structure and numerous agents.
Hypnotic cacophony apparent chaos,
Trumpet solos flash and rouse us.
To the tumultuous climax in full strain,
The final beats caress the brain.
An audience unite in thunderous applause,
To show jazz alive is a mighty cause.

AUGUST 1912

In August '12 there was such a flood,
That the Yare and Wensum were tinged with blood.
We all lost many of our sheep and goats,
To collect our provisions we used small boats.
Our potatoes and swedes rotted in the fields,
From the wheat and the barley there were such low yields.
For days our houses were clogged with silt,
Some of our dwellings had to be rebuilt.
But we pulled together and we didn't starve,
At Yuletide there was Norfolk turkey to carve.
Though many of us had been quite ill,
For the children we still had stockings to fill.

HAIKUS

Outside My Park

Hungry child in tears,
Deep, sunken eyes with flies,
Clings on to mother.

Entering My Park

The blast of traffic,
Diminishes to zero,
My head is caressed.

Inside My Park

Scented mauve flowers,
All kinds of beautiful beasts,
Frequent the peace space.

INSOMNIA

In the darkness there glows a man-made light,
That fills the endless hours of night.
The rhythmic ticking of the battery clock,
The distant voices they seem to mock.
I pull on shirt, some pants, some shoes,
Patter down the stairs and I muse,
Everything sounds much louder now,
From the streets the cries of a faraway row.
The lake is quiet, forlorn and black,
The moonless night and the solitary quack,
Of a disturbed duck, I shuffle by,
For a good night's sleep I feel I could die.

INVISIBLE

Through the brine and the barnacles and the soupy murk,
I peer around frames because that is my work.
My lifeblood's a cylinder, the bubbles issue forth,
There are fewer lovely fish in the seas of the north.
I inspect the giant towers for the nation's wealth,
By a life of constant motion I maintain my health.
If I surface too quickly I shall feel very sick,
The gases in my blood will make me sink like a brick.
I protect the supply for your heating and your buses,
It's a life of great danger but nobody fusses.

NEBRASKA

The fecund fields of amber grain,
Spread upward to the grassy plain.
Where the windpumps grind an eerie tune,
And time stands still in the heat of June.
The pitiless wind howls the winter through,
On a dead straight road I travel to you.
With the distant mountains and their bluish tinge,
And the roadside café on burgers to binge.
Sit many a traveller in brown-chequered shirts,
Who put up with the pain however much it hurts.
From the saddle and the cab peer screwed up eyes,
See the land of plenty as the American prize.

SAVIOUR

From the dust of the stars You willed to form us,
At the birth of Your son was a heavenly chorus.
Before simple shepherds who heard great tidings,
And the sages of the East on camels riding.
You came to earth to redeem the destitute,
The beggars and tax collectors, lepers and prostitutes.
You gave new life to the daughter of Jairus,
After four days dead You raised Your friend Lazarus.
You chose the pain so that we could walk free,
Sin and death defeated while nailed to a tree.
By glorious resurrection you gave us hope,
Through faith and love in You we can cope,
With the hardships and trials that lie in the path,
Your Holy Spirit envelopes us like a spiritual bath.
Dear Jesus we're so glad that your blood has bought,
The hungry people whom without you are nought.

THE MARKET

In the shadow of the mighty Parish Church,
As the clock chimes down the hours,
Nestles the Friday market,
Between Helen's Pantry and the Town Hall.
The weight of the honeydew melons,
And shiny black aubergines,
"Kilo of tomatoes please."
"Thank you." The crisp, crumpled paper bag,
In my clasping hand as I meander,
Through the throng towards the clothes stall.
Jenny is the vendor there,
Sunlight catches her long, hennaed hair,
A turquoise blouse with trimming,
On arms and hem and floral skirt,
Billowed by the wind from the alleys.
"How's it going, Jenny?" I smile.
"T'was busy last Friday but this week dead."
I feel glad it's not winter.
Have seen her here with fingerless gloves,
Holding a mug of hot soup to her lips.
I buy a fruit juice from a nearby stall,
She accepts it gratefully with twinkling eye.

UPSIDE DOWN (FOR CHILDREN)

In a land on the underside of the world,
Lives a wide-eyed bear that sleeps,
Twenty-two hours a day,
To digest the leaves she eats.
All the tourists love her,
Because she is so cute,
But she likes to be left in peace,
Close her eyes and dream,
Of Mum, who loved her but is gone,
Where the natives say you go,
When your loving heart is spent,
Your tummy's tired, your eyes are sore.
The sun beats down on the shy little bear,
The dusty wind blows and groans,
Dries her to the bone,
But the ranger will take care of her,
When the visitors have gone.

STARS (Flash Fiction)

I dislike my cousin Ricky. He picks his nose and slurps his tea. When I speak to him he simply grunts. To me he seems morose and he doesn't like strangers. His spectacles are always dirty, likewise his greasy pubescent hair.

Mother dotes on him. Soft boiled free-range eggs and soggy soldiers at lunchtime, crumpets and chit-chat at tea.

One churchyard dark night, still as death, Ricky jerks his head.

"D'you want to go outside, it's clear?"

"Yes alright."

I stand shivering in the garden. He points to the sky and smiles. Ricky never smiles.

"The Constellation Orion," he says. "Betelgeuse, Bellatrix." His fingers wafts downwards. "Alnitak, Alnilam, Mintaka, The Belt.

"Saiph, Rigel ... 900 light years away. The Nebula under the Belt."

Ricky proceeds to name all the stars in Leo, Ursa Major and Cassiopeia.

This preceded many cold but happy interludes stargazing. Gradually my attitude to Ricky changed.

ESTHER AND THE BULGE

SCENE 1

9.30pm on a Monday evening in May.

Barry and Joanne enter a supermarket. They take a trolley and begin shopping.

Joanne: All we seem to do these days is work, sleep and eat, Barry, there must be more to life than this.

Barry resignedly picks up a pack of beers.

Joanne: Do you really need all that beer, love?
Barry: Just at the moment, yes, I haven't moaned about you eating all that chocolate.
Joanne: We need some more air freshener, how about a plug-in one?
Barry: O.K.

They reach the babyware area.

Joanne: Barry, I can't stand this any more, all these baby products. When are we going to have a baby?

A tear wells up in her eye. Barry puts his arm around her.

Barry: We will one day, mark my words. The IVF will work one day.
Joanne: You ... You always say that but it never does.
Barry: I don't know what to say any more. We've talked till we're blue in the face about it. What can I say? We'll have a cuddle in front of the telly when we get in.
Joanne: It's always the same Barry.

They pay for their shopping and exit into the car park, Barry carrying the shopping.

SCENE 2

In the car park.

Joanne: I can hear crying, Barry.
Barry: Yeh, it seems to be coming from that skip.
Joanne: Let's go and take a look.

They look in the skip.

Joanne: My god, Barry, it's an abandoned baby. Shall we take it home just for safe keeping for a while?
Barry: Could land us in hot water if the mother's traced. We'd better hurry up before someone sees us.

They hurry to their car and get inside. An old man walks past the car but may not have seen the baby in Joanne's arms ... After a minute's driving ...

Barry: Jo, wouldn't it be easier if we just took the poor mite to hospital?
Joanne: But you want a child as much as I do, don't you?
Barry: Yes, but John and Faye Cooper are bound to be looking through the curtains even at this time of night and they'll see us carrying a baby into the house without a pushchair and you aren't pregnant.
Joanne: Oh Barry, let's keep the baby.
Barry: Trouble is all the neighbours read the *Argus* and what if somebody saw the baby before us and told the police and it's straight in the *Argus*?
Joanne: I have an idea Barry, why don't we make a false ... or even lots of false bulges that I can wear under my dress that'll make it look as if I'm getting more pregnant?
Barry: God you're off your trolley. What about the kid crying at night, the Coopers are bound to hear it?
Joanne: Barry, we're childless and some cruel person has put a new-born baby in a skip!
Barry: You mean our morals are much higher than theirs.
Joanne: Yes!
Barry: Won't cut much ice with The Bill when they call round.

Joanne: We could put the cot in the loft until she gets bigger. The Coopers might not hear because of the insulation.
Barry: So you're going to wear a bulge until it's time for a home delivery and the Coopers notice no midwife or Health Visitors turn up.
Joanne: We can say you delivered her.
Barry: Bloody hell! I don't know about bonding with a child to cement a marriage but this is going to split us up.
Joanne: Give it a chance Barry. I heard the Coopers are moving soon and the other side are always stoned out their brains anyway.
Barry: I don't think we'll end up in the same jail, but if you're that desperate I'll give it a try for us. But it means you'll have to be home seven days a week unless I am and you work full-time with your artificial bulge.
Joanne: We'll work it out, Barry.
Barry: I suppose you'll be asking for maternity leave.
Joanne: I expect so.
Barry: God I dunno about Baldrick in *Blackadder* but this plan takes the biscuit.

They pull up at home. Gingerly, Joanne carries the infant indoors. Barry scurries indoors.

SCENE 3

Barry: No lights on next door, that's a relief.
Joanne: How old do you think this babby is, Barry?
Barry: You'd know better than me, try feeling the top of her head.
Joanne: She must be quite young, weeks maybe. She's just so cute.
Barry: I'll go into town tomorrow Jo, and buy some baby clothes and nappies and stuff. I don't want you to go yet, it's just too risky until the story is out of the papers. We'll need a pushchair quickly, we can't be carrying her round.
Joanne: What about a name for her, Barry?
Barry: I'm going to get a beer from the fridge.
Joanne: No, really Barry, I like biblical names, maybe Esther Ruth.

Barry: Sounds O.K. to me, but we need to get her settled down in bed before she starts crying again. I'll just drink this and put the cot in the loft.
Joanne: You'll need the stepladder, love. I'll carry Esther and the cot.
Barry: Be careful. That cot's heavier than it looks. Damn it! I've just thought there's no light in the loft. I'll get my torch from the car.

Barry goes out to the car. The Coopers next door have just arrived home.

John: Hello Barry, are you O.K.?
Barry: Hello John. Hello Faye. Very well thanks.

Hurriedly he opens the boot and collects the torch and scampers indoors.

John: Lovely night.

The Coopers disappear indoors.

Barry: Just coming Jo, I'll get the extension lead from the cupboard under the stairs and the table lamp from the lounge and we'll have it fixed.

He does so and joins Jo on the landing just as Esther starts to cry.

Barry: Damn it! We'll have to get moving, the Coopers have just come in.
Joanne: What about a little beaker of Ribena? That might calm her down a little.
Barry: Can't we get her in the cot first?

Barry puts up the stepladder and climbs it and pushes up the loft entrance. He takes the cot from Jo while carrying the torch.

Barry: This is a going to be a bloody tight squeeze getting this cot in with one hand. Tell you what, let's fix up the light first.
Joanne: Oh hurry Barry, there's a good man. I'll pop down to get some Ribena with Esther and come back and hand you the cot.

She does so. Barry plugs the extension lead in on the landing and places the table lamp on one of the cross members in the loft. He comes down and switches on the power.

Barry: Da, da! Let there be light.

Jo returns upstairs.

Joanne: Esther's quietened down a bit but we need milk powder early tomorrow.
Barry: I'll deal with that, let me hold her a minute.

He does.

Barry: O.K., the cot.

Barry struggles to get the cot through the aperture, in which Jo has put a little sheet, blankets and a toy, but he gets the cot into the loft.

Barry: We've got a slight problem love, the cot doesn't stretch between two cross members. I'll need to get a piece of board from the shed.
Joanne: Shall I bring Esther up then and put her in and then hold the cot still?
Barry: You're a top woman, careful on that ladder and stepping in the loft.

Barry comes down and goes to fetch some board. Jo climbs the ladder with Esther in her arms. She only just manages to get into the loft with Esther. She places Esther in the cot and squatting down manages to keep it level. Barry returns with the board and puts it in place with Jo's help. Esther settles down and Jo and Barry go to bed.

Barry: If we use some chicken wire and put papier mâché over it, let it dry and tape up the sharp edges it should make a good bulge for you love.
Joanne: Perhaps, but we'll need soft straps to hold it in place. I don't know how long I'm gonna put up with it.
Barry: With a bit of luck you won't have to wear it indoors unless we get visitors. We could say to Maggie that we're on holiday if she wants to come. I doubt she'll come all the way from Southampton to find out.

Joanne: It's sudden visitors that worry me, and keeping Esther quiet while they're here. Oh Barry this is going to be such a struggle, let's have a cuddle and settle down.

SCENE 4

The next morning Barry returns with a car laden with baby shopping. Mr Cooper is clipping his side of the hedge.

John: Morning Barry.
Barry: Uh . . . Morning John.
John: Got a lot of shopping there. Excuse me being nosey, but what's with the pushchair?
Barry: Jo's pregnant, I thought I'd get some supplies.
John: Congratulations mate, after all this time. Oh, on the subject of babies we heard some crying from your place last night.
Barry: Yes, we were babysitting 'til quite late for my cousin in Guildford. They were having adult baptism and a social and it went on late.
John: Good show mate, getting some practice in.

Barry bites his lip and hurries inside.

Barry: Jo.
Joanne: Here love.
Barry: Now we're really in the lurch, I had to tell John Cooper you're pregnant. I wish he'd mind his own business and another thing crossed my mind. When we go to get a Birth Certificate they'll notice that Esther's well developed. I want out of this.
Joanne: Darling, think of all the poor children in Africa, they never have a Birth Certificate. Esther's been great this morning too.
Barry: Jo, we're living in bloody Mitcham not Timbuktu!
Joanne: Well, if it's any consolation, I've finished the papier mâché mould and it's drying. If you could fasten the ties.
Barry: That was quick love.
Joanne: Remember, I used to do this stuff at art college. By the way I'd like to go out in the front garden and tidy up a bit after

tea. Would you mind looking after Esther later? I'm already fed up with these four walls.
Barry: Can't you go out the back. There's less chance of the Coopers being nosey, they don't go out there so much.
Joanne: Alright, if you wish but try not to fret so much. There's a jacket potato in the oven and some tuna salad in the fridge.

SCENE 5

That Evening. Joanne picks up the papier mâché bulge.

Joanne: Time to try it out.
Barry: O.K. I'll fasten the ties.
Joanne: God, it feels funny. Good job you bought the maternity blouse.
Barry: Yeh, I spent a fortune this morning.
Joanne: Esther might need a nappy change if she wakes up. She's just had some milk and I winded her. If she cries a lot I'll be in tout-suite.

Jo goes to the shed, picks up a trowel and kneeler pad and begins to do some light weeding in a flower bed. She hums quietly to herself. Next door is a rotary washing line with washing hanging on it.

Faye Cooper: Congratulations!

Joanne looks up with a lump in her throat.

Joanne: Uh, thank you, I'm expecting a daughter.
Faye: Good luck to you. Our daughter has been very wayward. She was alright in her early teens but she's been quite bad lately. I won't say more than that.
Joanne: How's your son?
Faye: Oh, we're very proud of him, he's in the Merchant Navy still. Always wanted to be in that or the Royal Navy. We don't see much of either of them. Annette only lives two miles away but we haven't seen her for six months. Ah well, you can but try.

Mrs Cooper trudges in with a basketful of washing. Jo works as long as she can and returns to the kitchen.

Joanne: She didn't mention anything about my belly suddenly getting bigger.
Barry: Well done. I've changed Esther's nappy. Might be best that we put her in her cot now. I'll do it, Jo, you relax a bit.

Barry goes up to the loft and puts Esther in her cot. He pulls his back slightly bending down in the loft. This distracts his attention from turning off the power on the landing.

Barry: I hurt my back a bit up there love.
Joanne: There's some Ralgex in the bathroom cupboard. Lie down for a while with your knees up.

SCENE 6

Jo and Barry relax for a couple of hours before bed.

Barry: I'll have to get back to work tomorrow.
Joanne: We'll need some more chicken wire some time, love. Enough to make a bigger bulge.
Barry: You're really determined aren't you?
Joanne: Yes, I want us to be happy.

They are just about to go to bed when the doorbell rings. Barry answers it. Before him stand a policeman and a bedraggled looking woman perhaps in her early twenties.

Policeman: Good evening sir.
Barry: Uh, good evening how can I help you?
Policeman: May I assume you are the owner of this blue Ford Fiesta, sir.
Barry: Uh, yes.
Policeman: We have a witness to you carrying a very young child to this car at about 2130 hours on Monday evening. This young woman has declared herself to be the mother of that child.

At this moment John Cooper appears on the other side of the hedge.

John: What's happening? Barry, there's smoke coming out of your loft window, can't you smell it?

The policeman, Barry and the young woman look up.

Policeman: I'll call the fire brigade at once, sir.
Barry: Yes you do that but I wanna go in. They may get here too late.

Barry sprints upstairs, carrying a torch up the stepladder and into a developing shroud of thick smoke. He grabs Esther and suffering pain brings her down the ladder where Jo is standing crying.

Barry: Switch that cable off!

Jo switches the power off.

Joanne checks the child's pulse and breathing.

Joanne; I think she's still alive. I'll call for an ambulance.
Barry: No. The copper will do that.

Meanwhile John Cooper is scowling over the hedge.

John: Annette! Is that you Annette? What the hell are you doing there?
Annette (through tears): It's my baby Dad.
John: What bloody baby? I'm coming over there.
Policeman: Would you mind leaving it to me, sir, until this is sorted.
Barry arrives at the door with Esther in his arms.

Barry: She's still alive officer.

Joanne disappears indoors in a rage and crying.

Policeman: An ambulance and fire crew are on their way, sir. You will be required to make statements. Because it is likely you have saved the child's life twice there may be mitigating circumstances.

John Cooper storms up the drive towards Annette just as Joanne arrives at the front door with a large bucket of water. She hurls the water over Annette and John gets soaked too.

Joanne: There you are you bitch, you dumped a child and we are childless! You can arrest me policeman, I've had enough!

Lightning Source UK Ltd.
Milton Keynes UK
UKOW041858120313

207534UK00001B/2/P